I0520310

Visit us on the web at swordsedgepublishing.ca
and swordsedge.ca

Table of Contents

Introduction

Sword Noir. I've been using the term a lot. I think I may be the only one doing so.

This collection exists in a large part because of a game Sword's Edge Publishing (let's just call it SEP, okay?) will be releasing called *Sword Noir*, which is subtitled *A Role-Playing Game of Hardboiled Sword & Sorcery*. Just as this collection tells of the underworld and those dwelling on the fringes of society, *Sword Noir* looks at the kind of stories told in film noir and hard-boiled fiction, but with the back drop of sword & sorcery fantasy—as one might guess by the subtitle.

What is sword noir? I defined it for myself—and for the game—as follows:

Characters' morals are shifting at best and absent at worst. The atmosphere is dark and hope is frail or completely absent. Violence is deadly and fast. The characters are good at what they do, but they are specialists. Trust is the most valued of commodities–life is the cheapest. Grim leaders weave labyrinthine plots which entangle innocents. Magic exists and can be powerful, but it takes extreme dedication to learn, extorts a horrible price, and is slow to conjure.

Now not all the stories in this collection meet that definition exactly. I don't think rigid adherence to any definition is a good way to write fiction, but this definition helped me to envisage sword noir while I developed the game. It also helped me to differentiate, in my mind, what sets it apart from sword & sorcery.

But honestly, it's not about the definition. It's about the voice. From the earliest of these stories, I was trying to find a different voice, a different point of view from which to tell sword & sorcery stories. I'm a bigger fan of Fritz Leiber than J.R.R. Tolkien. I'd rather read Glen Cook than Stephen Donaldson. I prefer David Gemmell to David Eddings. All these writers work(ed) in sword &

sorcery—more or less, remember, rigid adherence not necessarily good. They also all have a very distinctive voice.

You'll see, in these stories, me trying to develop my voice, trying to work a bit of the lyricism of Leiber into the realism of Cook and the cynical idealism of Gemmell. As I read more hard-boiled fiction, that began to inform my writing. That voice I'm trying to find continues to elude me, only because it continues to evolve. The latest stories I'm working on may sound similar to "Flotsam Jewel" or "For Simple Coin", but there are noticeable differences.

I'm even working on a first person short story, something from which many editors and critique group partners warn writers away.

I'll take the risk. It's time to evolve.

The Spear: A Tale of Hadrapole

This story goes way back, back to a point at which I don't think I was that good of a writer. It's been polished, fixed, and had a facelift, so I'm not ashamed to present it now. This is an important story for me because it touches on almost all the aspects of sword noir that I later defined to help focus my writing and now my game design. It was also one of the first stories to present Hadrapole, the setting for three out of the four stories in this collection.

Hadrapole was meant to be an alternate Constantinople in that it was a cosmopolitan centre of civilization and commerce. Unlike Constantinople, it was not the centre of a massive political and military empire. And it never fell. Well, not yet.

Think of it as Constantinople by way of Lankhmar.

Such a setting worked well with the stories I wanted to tell—stories about the dark underbelly where the fringe dwellers lived. Chang, the main character in the Spear, is a hero just as are Calum and Caspan Trey, whom you'll meet later. He's not exactly an anti-hero. He's not being drawn into the story against his will. He's not fighting it. He just happens to dwell in the darkness, away from the bright light of day. Maybe he doesn't act heroic, but that's because he's not stupid. He's a professional.

I can't say exactly what drew me into the underworld. I had not, until I started writing what later became sword noir, read crime or detective fiction. I knew of hard-boiled detective fiction, I had heard of Sam Spade and Phillip Marlowe, but I had never made their acquaintance. It was, in fact, these stories that lead me to watch film noir, as they seemed so similar in tone and content to that which I hoped to write. Those movies led me to the novels and stories that inspired them as I explored where my writing might take me.

So "the Spear" is a kind of artefact, one that has been recovered and restored. If you have visited South Korea—where I lived for a few years—you may have been to one of the castles, fortresses or palaces that dot the country. Seoul itself has at least three. None of them are authentic. They've all been rebuilt recently, some because they were destroyed by the Japanese some because the Koreans would rather have something that looks good than something that is authentic. That's this story. It's been rebuilt because I would rather present you a good story than a story that authentically illustrates my skills in the past.

THE SPEAR

A Tale of Hadrapole

I

Chang didn't know the name of the place, and he didn't particularly care. Below street level, it sat on a block about three streets up from the wharves. He found it outside the walls, in the Stonedocks—the berths used by smugglers and pirates, nominally controlled by Hadrapole, but really controlled by no one. Neither of the Night Guilds, not the Blackhands nor the Mashaam, dominated the Docks. Both tried, and this invariably led to some of the bodies found every morning in the streets, alleys and shore of the Docks.

He guessed the building was supposed to be a tavern— maybe a brothel or an inn, if anyone made a distinction between the two in that place. Chang knew the Stonedocks well; he had done plenty of business there. That day he had arranged to meet one of the Hands. A messenger had left a note with his landlord. Chang lived in Twelve Shadow Walk, abutting the Pale Gate, in the shadows of that gate's twelve towers. The landlord had no clue about Chang's business, but he probably thought him some sort of merchant. That belief had apparently changed after the visit from the Hands' messenger.

In the tavern, the stink of sour beer and spoiled food assailed Chang's nostrils, worse even than he had expected. He almost rapped his head on a beam. That surprised him. He rarely had to duck his head in the buildings of Hadrapole. That low ceiling caught the smoke that drifted lazily about, cast off by both torches and candles. The mid-day bells had not yet sounded in the city, and already the darkness of the blackest midnight had descended in the tavern.

Chang took a seat near a window, with his back to a wall. Many of the patrons, all of them dirty, slovenly, miserable racks, watched him. Chang didn't care. People would always stare. Few other men with his features walked the streets of Hadrapole. The city was cosmopolitan, but among the impoverished and destitute—which would be the kindest name for the denizens of that hole— xenophobia remained common. They hated foreigners. To a one, they all forgot that their roots lay in foreign lands. The original tribes that had inhabited the lands around Hadrapole had been exterminated or assimilated by the Empire.

The rich and the merchants hated foreigners also—Chang knew that well—but they hid it better.

A thin, cadaverous man, with lank, greasy hair approached Chang's table. The man wore tattered and dirty clothing. The stench of the tavern seemed to increase as he moved closer.

"What you doing here?" the man asked. "This place belongs to the Blackhands."

"I am here on business," Chang said, his voice flat. "Do I know you?"

"I'm with the Hands."

Chang sniffed. "You look barely better than a finger with a dirty nail."

The man drew out a thin knife. It had darkened wood for a handle and a blade that didn't really deserve the name. Looking from it back up into the man's eyes, Chang allowed a slight smile to creep onto his face.

He gestured to the pathetic attempt at a weapon. "Put that away."

The man took a step closer, brandishing the knife before him. "You had better get out of here, Squinty, or you're going to get hurt."

Chang wrestled with his options. Should he make an example of the insolent little turd or should he simply disarm him as a warning? It might not be wise to insult the Hands, but would the Hands consider killing such this annoyance an insult? Who knew if he were really with the Hands.

"Get out of here, Karlos," the man behind the bar shouted. "You don't know who that Squinty is?"

"He's going to be dead he don't get out of here," the turd, apparently named Karlos, said.

The bartender chortled. "Only person going to be dead is you. That's Chang the Spear. If he's here, the Hands probably sent for him."

Chang had never heard himself called 'the Spear', and he wasn't sure if he had told anyone the translation of his name in the local language. Either someone had learned its meaning or serendipity had struck. Whichever the case, it mattered not at all.

Karlos the Turd looked at Chang. The knife dropped slightly, no longer threatening, but still present. Karlos stood on unsteady feet, leaning and lilting, regaining his posture only to lose it again. His eyes couldn't seem to focus on Chang, and his brow knit in concentration. Chang decided it would be rather beneath his dignity to kill this human waste.

The door banged open before Karlos could make any decision. He whirled to look. Chang had a perfect view of the door. Four men, tall burly fellows with scars and clubs, entered the tavern. Karlos took a step back, bringing him a step closer to Chang.

"Everybody out of here," one of the men said. He pointed to the bartender. "You too, Hakel"

Karlos took a hesitant step toward the door. He put away his makeshift knife, hiding it somewhere within the folds of his tattered tunic. The men at the door ushered everyone out, their words and actions lacking consideration or kindness. Chang rose, but the man who had spoke shook his head and pointed to Chang's chair. Chang sat down. The bartender, the one called Hakel, left last. The speaking man gave Hakel a small purse as the bartender passed him, and Chang could see the glee grow on Hakel's face.

Chang felt no surprise at how quickly the tavern had emptied, since there had been so few in attendance. The four men remained by the door, now closed. They all took seats. They spoke to each other in low voices, and they scrutinized Chang without subtlety.

He heard nothing behind him for many heartbeats. He watched the men at the door watch him. His attention rested there, so when the voice spoke, almost in his ear, he was startled. He didn't jump or react in any way save perhaps a quickly drawn breath.

"Thank you for coming, Master Chang," the voice said.

Chang turned and saw a man shorter than himself, dressed in well-made, if not ostentatious clothing, unsoiled and without a single tear. The man who wore it had no beard and a clean-shaven head. His eyes were small, as were his lips. In the dim light, Chang couldn't make out the color of the man's eyes.

"You would be Martos?" Chang asked.

"Yes, I'm Martos, Denfather of the Blackhands." The man took a chair at Chang's table, even though Chang had not offered one. "I really didn't expect you would come."

Chang raised an eyebrow. "Then why did you ask me?"

Martos winked. "In case you would. It seems I made the proper choice."

"And here?" Chang looked around at the dirty, stinking interior of the tavern.

"You've been in the area before, you're known to come to the Stonedocks." Martos gestured to the men at the door. "Because of my men's' performance, it will be known you were meeting someone important, but no one will know who."

"Then you have considered my offer?"

Martos grunted—almost a chuckle. "I didn't believe it when I heard it. I guess I believe it now, since you're here. I'd like to hear it from you though."

"I want to join the Hands," Chang said

A tight grin slowly reached Martos' lips and he shook his head. He looked to his men, then back at Chang. His breath smelt like mint and his body smelt like lilacs. He must be a rich man.

"And we want you, especially now," Martos said. "If you complete one task for me, I'll not only offer you membership in the Hands, I'll make you my lieutenant. You can choose whichever district you would like to run."

"One task? That is all?"

"You haven't heard the task yet." Martos chuckled. "You know Arnmir, the Sorcerer?" Martos waited until Chang nodded. "He's been amassing a fair clutch of gold, and he's been teaching some of the Mashaam wizards. Their power is increasing, and threatening us around the Docks."

Chang grunted acknowledgement. He knew all that, though perhaps he shouldn't. He knew which families gained influence in the council, and that Arnmir had helped them. He also knew that those families had ties to the Mashaam, through which the Mashaam had gained access to Arnmir for their wizards and witches. Chang could well guess what Martos wanted him to do.

"I can kill Arnmir."

Martos didn't speak. He watched Chang, who watched Martos' mouth. Chang saw the miniscule movements there, and the perspiration on the edge of Martos' scalp. Martos was surprised.

"Just like that?" Martos finally asked. "No talk of money or dangers?

Chang shrugged. "I need to get into your group. It has become too dangerous for a freelance to continue working. If this is the price, this is what I will do."

"Membership in the Hands won't be your only reward," Martos said. "There will be silver, and maybe a little gold. And once you have your own territory, there will be coin to gain there."

"Do you think that is where I can help you best?"

"And where do you think you could help?"

"As a freelance, I am in demand. I am also able to enter places most Hands could not and learn things the Hands rarely learn. If I become a Hand, all these things change."

"That's true." Martos tapped his forehead with his index finger. "And it is one reason why only you and I are meeting today."

"I beg your pardon, but it is not you and I." Chang placed his hands, palms down, on the table. "There are four pairs of eyes on us, and no matter how trusted your men are, others will know."

Martos leaned back in his chair. He rubbed his chin, and stared at Chang. Did he want to turn and look at those men at the door? Did he want to see if his men listened? Perhaps they did not, but they would see the two sitting together, and would tell others what they saw.

"What do we do about this?" Martos asked.

Chang sat back in his chair. "I will refuse your offer. You will leave here, not angry but perhaps frustrated. We will not be seen together again. At an appointed time, at an appointed place, I will meet you again, collect my fee and receive more orders."

"You'll be my secret weapon, is that it?" Martos asked.

"Would that not be best? It is for my safety that I have approached you, but it would be better for me to remain known as a freelance—even if there are dangers with that."

Martos inhaled loudly. "How long do you think you can keep up the masquerade?"

"I am not certain," Chang said. "Perhaps I will need to disappear, but I promise whatever the circumstance, I will remain useful to you."

"I'm sure you will," Martos said. "There is a back door here, and stairs inside of it leading to a small loft. In five days, two bells after sunset, I'll meet you there. That is, if Arnmir is dead."

Arnmir's gaze returned to Chang. "Then I must die."

"And how will you achieve this?"

"I have an elixir that simulates death," Arnmir said. "I will administer it to myself tonight. The word will go out tomorrow that I have been found dead, and you will have your meeting with Martos."

Chang frowned. "Will this not leave you vulnerable? What if they attempt to perform some rites, or to immolate your remains?"

"My two most trusted adepts will guard me. And I am certain you will not allow me to come to harm. You would certainly not allow the key to your ambitions to be lost."

Chang did not reply. He looked away from the wizard. Arnmir laughed.

"Yes, I know it is not out of love but out of ambition that you serve me," Arnmir said. "It is no matter. What is important is that you do serve me. And soon we will have both the Hands and the Mashaam under our control, and none will know it."

"And I will be master of both?" Chang asked.

"Not immediately, of course, but yes, you will. And soon, I will be able to control the Arcanum Guild. With the thieves and the wizards at our control, the merchants will be left little choice but to follow our dictates. The Council will be all but at my command. Hadrapole has not had a monarch since she left the Empire, but even if I haven't the name, I will be her prince."

Arnmir chewed his lower lip as he watched Chang. Chang said nothing.

"You may go," Arnmir said. "Tomorrow morning I will be dead. The elixir will not last long though. Serilo and Anasius will remove me from Hadrapole. Which way will draw the least attention?"

Chang did not immediately reply. He rubbed his cheek. He looked up after a long silence. "There is a ship I can hire. The captain will not ask about cargo. It is a short jaunt to the port at Qelavos. You can wait there, and I will return to meet with Martos. Once that is done, you can return however you wish."

Arnmir lifted his cup as though in salute. "Tomorrow night then. Serilo and Anasius will be expecting you. I doubt they will trust you, though."

"Few do."

Chang departed from the compound the same way he had entered it.

III

The two adepts, Serilo and Anasius, watched over their sleeping mentor. Many guests had visited that day, paying respects to Arnmir. A great outcry had greeted the report of his death, and when the rumor of poisoning reached the Arcanum Guild, they vowed they would find the culprit.

Three bells rang from Peril's Tower, marking the third hour since sunset. It had been only an hour since the last of the visitors had left. The adepts sat at a table eating a light meal, not two paces from the coffin in which their master lay. Only a small amount of food remained from the great banquet offered in honor of the wizard. It had been speedily prepared, but still exquisite.

The apprentices were not young men. Serilo had seen thirty winters, and Anasius was a mature twenty-eight. Both had the dark hair and dark eyes common in Hadrapole. They both came from good families, families which saw great possibilities for the two in the Arcanum Guild.

Serilo prepared to bite into a large chunk of pork when he froze. The food had not yet reached his mouth, which hung open. Seeing this, Anasius turned. A thin, dark figure stood by the coffin. The figure turned to face the adepts. Chang sighed as he looked at the two.

13

"I suppose the three of us will be forced to carry him," Chang said.

No word of greeting. No information about their destination or their passage. Business was business, especially in Hadrapole.

"We know some spells that will make his coffin lighter," Serilo said.

Chang tapped the coffin. "An illusion would be better."

Anasius scoffed. "No matter what illusion we cast, we will be carrying the coffin. Unless you believe it is less suspicious for two apprentice magi and a thief to be carrying a settee down the streets late at night."

"Well, then," Chang said, "shall we get to it?"

Serilo looked to Anasius, who rolled his eyes. The two rose and approached the coffin.

"Should we close it?" asked Chang.

"It doesn't matter," Serilo said. "The master is completely insensible. He won't be noticing anything like light and dark for a few hours longer."

Chang flexed his arms, then moved to the coffin. He took an end while Serilo and Anasius shared the other. The three hefted the coffin up. All three grunted with the effort.

"Just a moment, I have something that will make this situation less troublesome," Chang said.

He put his end of the coffin on the table, directly on the food. The other two men groaned in protest.

"Whatever it is, hurry," Anasius said. "The master is light, but his coffin is staggeringly heavy."

"I expect it is." Chang reached under his dark jacket.

Both of his hands extended, and he released two daggers. The daggers found throats. The two apprentices released their master's coffin and dropped. The coffin fell to the floor, onto Serilo.

The apprentice could do nothing as the coffin crashed into him, pinning his lower legs against the ground. He did not protest. His hands clutched at his throat, blood flowing from there and his mouth. Serilo died. Anasius lasted marginally longer, long enough to point at Chang and then die.

The toxin is slower than I was led to believe, and less effective. It was quite possible Anasius died of the cut to his throat rather than the poison on the dagger's blade.

Chang stepped over and looked at Arnmir. He had shifted in his coffin, but he had not woken. Chang put a hand on Arnmir's throat. He could feel no discernable pulse. The wizard didn't seem to breath.

"You certainly seem dead, but I know you are not," Chang said. "For my purposes, that is not acceptable. I apologize for my deception, but maybe ambition is not a good enough reason to serve."

Chang drew out a third dagger and drove it down into Arnmir's chest. The dagger also had poison on it, though Chang didn't believe that necessary.

Still, one had to be certain.

IV

The door swung open at the barest of touches. Chang stood and watched it. No one emerged. He stepped inside and looked about. It was darker inside the room than on the unlit streets. Chang closed the door. He did not wish to be outlined for anyone who might await within.

Feeling about, Chang found the stairs. He hoped that Martos had kept his word. It would be most unfortunate if he had killed the wizard Arnmir for no purpose. Chang listened at the stairs and heard nothing, but he believed he saw light at the top.

About three quarters of the way up, the stairs turned to the right. Chang looked around the corner, and saw the room at the top. Martos lay there, a single candle beside him. He had a jug which he clutched. He seemed to sleep.

Chang entered the room. Small, it had no furnishings. He sat down, across the candle from Martos. He watched the sleeping man, and it seemed to him that Martos did not really sleep. Maybe it was the rhythm of his breathing, or his eyes in their movement, or maybe it was just instinct, but Chang felt certain Martos did not slumber.

"Are you awake, Martos?" Chang asked.

Martos stirred. He pretended to waken, but Chang felt even more certain that this was feigned. Waiting to see if I'd strike at him while he slept? Probably. And did he expect some trap would kill Chang if he had tried to attack the sleeping Martos? That might make things more difficult.

Chang remained confident.

"Ah, Chang, are you late?" Martos rubbed his eyes.

"No."

Martos scratched his neck. He reached into his jerkin and drew out a small purse. He tossed it to Chang.

"Thirty currents, my friend, for a job well done. I was very impressed."

Chang stuffed the purse beneath his own jerkin. Martos watched his hand as it withdrew, empty. Chang wondered at Martos' suspicions. Then again, those without suspicion often found themselves dead.

"What is next for me?" Chang asked.

"I'm not sure yet, but I want you to keep your eyes on the Arcanum Guild," Martos said. "I think they know who was behind this."

"Do you think they will retaliate?"

"Perhaps, but not against me," Martos said. "They don't know who I am, and they could never get close enough anyway."

Chang rubbed his chin. "I will begin asking subtle questions in the right quarters. Also, we must decide how we will maintain contact without alerting anyone."

Martos stared into Chang's eyes for a few moments. He searched for something. Finally, he shrugged. "Yes, we will." Martos picked up the jug and raised it to Chang. "To our alliance, and to your future."

Martos' head tipped back as he drank from the jug. Chang surged forward, knocking over the candle in his haste. His left hand grasped Martos' throat as his right hand drove a dagger up through Martos' jaw and into his brain. He withdrew the dagger and punched it into Martos' heart. The Hand denmaster swung the jug at Chang, and it hit. Even as Chang fell back, Martos died.

Chang got to his knees. The candle had rolled into a pile of old straw, dirty and covered with refuse. He hesitated. Had Martos laid a trap?

He waited only a heartbeat. Nothing. He turned and descended the stairs. He did not wait to listen for anyone at the base of the stairs, but moved quickly, bloody dagger still in his hand.

Chang met no one at the bottom of the stairs. The light from the fire illuminated the stairwell and the door. He rushed out and disappeared easily into the Stonedocks as the tavern burned behind him.

V

Philotos would like to have been in bed. Most civilized men were. The Urban Tribune looked at the multitude of papers before him. He had reports about the Imperial Navy massing near trade routes, and of the Vast Kingdoms advocating a crusade against the godless, forgetting that Hadrapole probably had more gods and priests than any other damn hole in the world. Beside these reports rested another notice from the Prefects stating that they might be unable to pay the legion until they gathered greater revenues.

Always the same, the reports and notices of gloom and doom always kept him awake at nights and in the end amounted to nothing. These were not the threats about which he should worry.

Unfortunately, he could only answer these threats.

If the Empire thought it could bully Hadrapole into trade concessions, it had forgotten that Hadrapole had a bigger navy and better sailors. If the Vast Kingdoms should decide to unite and attack Hadrapole, they would dash themselves to pieces against her walls. Those would never be breached. And if the Prefects preferred to line their pockets and buy influence in the Council to paying the legions, well, he just might let a maniple or two of his men loose in the city after he gave them that news. Just one night of rioting should suffice.

Those problems all had solutions. His greatest worry was that stupid bastard Arnmir, trying to gain power among the Night Guilds. One just simply did not do that, not if one held a seat on the Council. Though not a law, everyone on the Council knew and accepted that. Of course, examples seemed eternally necessary.

And then there was Martos, him and his Blackhands. The Hands had gained the upper hand against the Mashaam. Two Night Guilds in balance helped maintain order. Criminal monopolies tended to induce arrogance. If Arnmir were to be done away with, Martos would need to go also. That should restore the equilibrium. Of course, it might also spark a naked struggle for power that could bring blood back to the streets. One always walked such a thin rope in Hadrapole.

He didn't hear him enter, but he never did. Philotos was certain no man could enter his home without permission, safe in the bosom of the barracks compound of the Civic Legion, but that man always did. It was one of the reasons Philotos employed him.

"Have you finished already, Chang?" Philotos asked.

"Both Arnmir and Martos are gone." Chang stood near the table at which Philotos sat.

"Are there any more that need to be silenced?" Philotos asked. "Will there be questions asked?"

Chang shook his head. "There will be no questions."

Philotos scratched his brow and looked at Chang. His eyes were red, and his face, always a strange shade, seemed even paler. He hadn't shaved recently, and that was odd for Chang. Philotos went over to a cabinet and took out a purse. He tossed it to Chang, who deftly caught it.

"There's enough in there that you can retire if you wish," Philotos said.

Chang slid the purse beneath his dark jacket. "I don't."

Philotos wanted to grin, but he held it in. "Then maybe you would like to take a little trip?"

"To the Vast Kingdoms? Perhaps have a discussion with some priests who think a crusade is a good idea?"

"No, I don't think you'd be very welcome there. A courier of mine has been intercepted and robbed of something quite important to me. I need you to find it and return it."

"Would the Night Guilds be so brazen?" Chang asked.

"No one knew the courier's employer, and I thought none knew the cargo," Philotos said. "While you find the item, I will be cleaning house."

"What can you tell me?"

"The item is a large, red jewel, not like anything you have likely seen." Philotos picked up one of the many papers on his desk and handed it to Chang. "This is all we know at the moment."

Chang exhaled slowly and then rose.

"You don't have to do it this night," Philotos said. "Get some rest."

Chang paused. A small smile reached his face. "Maybe I will."

Philotos wasn't sure what the statement meant, and he had no chance to ask Chang. As quietly as he had come, Chang left. Philotos looked back at the reports on his table.

Maybe I will be able to get some sleep tonight.

- the end -

Flotsam Jewel

This is the first story in which I was actually considering the themes and the sources that inspired me. I had read precious little crime fiction at the time, but I had read Elmore Leonard, and I was trying to meld Glen Cook's grim and gritty sense with Leonard's realism and pat dialogue, folding it all into my own style. The success of that attempt is for you to judge, not me.

This is also the first story that got me favourable comments from and even the chance to re-submit to John O'Neil at *Black Gate*. Being pretty much the only heroic fantasy print journal out there, Black Gate has always been my Grail—it's that for which I quest. Maybe it is just me, but getting a personalized rejection, especially with suggestions, is a win. It's not selling a story, but it is darn close. As it turned out, this started a relationship with Mr. O'Neil. *Black Gate* remains the first place to which I send my work—when they are accepting submissions that is. It finally led to a sale. I finally got my Grail. Unfortunately, that story isn't out yet, so it's not in this collection.

Getting the comments from Mr. O'Neil really helped to advance the story-telling, but I didn't fix enough in the next draft to meet his standards. Re-working continued with every rejection, because I now believed this was a story that could be good enough for the pay markets.

Among his points, Mr. O'Neill suggested that the story needed something to differentiate it from all the other stories out there. That became the setting. In the only review for this story that I could find, the setting was called out as one of its best elements. Flotsam was different. And in adding Flotsam, I made it more than just background. In many ways, Flotsam impacts on the story. It is almost an ally to the hero. It's a place to which I've planned to return, but so far, that story—which would be part of a novel or perhaps a novella—has not moved past the planning stage.

This story finally did see publication, but the issue in which it appeared turned out to be *Forgotten Worlds* last. That took some wind out of my sails. It's nice to get paid for the story—it's kind of the point if one is attempting to become "professional," but that is a whole other discussion—but if no one actually reads it, is there a point?

Here's another little bit of "inside baseball:" selling a reprint is even harder than selling a new story. It doesn't matter that the story appeared in a journal from the United Kingdom, the last issue of which, and one that did not, in fact, receive wide distribution. It is literally a buyers' market, and unless one has name recognition, a resale is a very, very long shot. Including the story in this collection is a chance to get it in front of a few more eyes.

FLOTSAM JEWEL

The building's undulations lulled Calum into a semi-trance. He sat in a chair on the roof of the Golden Boar, a gambling hall that masqueraded as a brothel, booted feet resting on the ledge. Like every other structure in Flotsam, the Boar floated in what had once been a harbor, outside the walls of Hadrapole.

Heavy footfalls echoing up the staircase broke into Calum's thoughts. He put his hand on the dagger he hid in his boot, the only weapon he carried that day. Who would have business so early at the dive in which he had diced?

Cresting the stairs, Mandas the Grunt—a good head taller than Calum and hairy like a bear—sniffed and grimaced. "What the Twelve Hells are you smoking, Calum?"

If the man hadn't worked for the Blackhands, one of the city's two criminal gangs—collectively known as the Night Guilds—Calum would have offered a rude reply. The Grunt's odor cut through the stink of smoke and Calum's *rolled*—a thin cigar concocted from his own collection of herbs. While he had muscle and grit, the Grunt lacked even a wisp of independent thought. He could've been a thug or a doorpost, and fate had made him a thug.

"Just trying to clear my head, Mandas." Calum couldn't risk calling him the Grunt. With no standing in either of the Night Guilds, Calum had no connections or friends to protect him, even against a pitifully connected walking tree trunk like the Grunt.

"Clearing your head, is it?" Without waiting for an invitation, Mandas sat at Calum's table. "What's to clear?"

Calum showed Mandas his dice before sliding them into their padded pouch. "Been dicing and drinking."

He didn't add that he had been losing. The night's gambling had left him considering filching a purse to cover his losses that night. His dice had offered no help.

Lucky dragon bone my ass.

"So you need work?" The smile on Mandas' face made Calum worry. It looked too much like a leer.

Calum scratched at his stubbled cheek. Mandas wasn't his friend. The Blackhands certainly weren't his friends. Why hire him? "What are you offering?"

"I need something collected. I figured you'd need the work."

Mandas the Grunt was a real boot-tread for Josak, the local boss for the Blackhands. What worried Calum was that since Mandas wasn't collecting, that meant Josak didn't want his own involved.

"Who's got what, and who wants it?"

"You know Tanos Six-Toes?"

Tanos worked for the Mashaam, the other major Night Guild. He had lost four toes in a fight with a whore. No one could actually explain *how* he had lost the toes. The two Night Guilds warred incessantly, and if Calum got between them, the scavengers wouldn't find much to pick off his bones.

"You know I can't touch one of the Mashaam," Calum said.

Mandas' leer widened. "How would they find out? I mean, if Tanos isn't around to tell them and all."

"I damn well can't kill one of the Mashaam." Calum surged to his feet. He didn't want to anger Mandas, but he felt insulted. How stupid did they think he was?

Mandas drew out a purse and dropped it on the table. It landed heavily, sending up the sound of metallic rattling. "That's silver in there, seventy-five pieces of minted Hadrapole silver."

Calum started to salivate. He rubbed his mouth and chin. "What do you need from Six-Toes?"

"There's a jewel, a big one, reddish colored but not like anything you've seen before," Mandas said. "Josak wants it. For some reason, he figures you'd be able to get it. Whatever else you find, you keep, along with that seventy-five."

If they offered him silver, the job was worth gold. How far could he push it? "If I'm hitting one of the Mashaam, and Josak wants to remain outside of it all, I'll want gold."

Mandas nodded. "Yeah, Josak figured you might. He'll pay you a bonus of fifty gold Hadrapole currents if you can get the jewel to him in three days. Any later than that, and no bonus. He'll still want the jewel."

Calum knew taking the money could get him killed. Walking away, though, also had its risks and offered no gold. He snatched up the purse. "Right, I'll get you your jewel, and in less than three days."

Without saying anything more, he stuffed the purse under his jerkin. He walked to the stairs then paused.

"Where do I find you when this is done?"

Mandas the Grunt leaned back in his chair. "Don't worry, Calum, we'll find you."

Descending the stairs, Calum figured he had just got hims0elf killed. Still, his life couldn't be worth much more than fifty gold currents.

Calum collapsed into the cushioned chair. It was the only luxury in an otherwise austere and bare abode. Little light penetrated the wooden slats of the shutters. His home consisted of two rooms, one for sleeping and the other for everything else. The hovel rested against one of the seawalls of Flotsam, a collection of old, wrecked boats and ships, tarred and nailed together to offer some protection. During storms though, waves would crest the walls and deluge the hovel. Still, the floor didn't leak and that was some small blessing.

In a straight-backed wooden chair sat Elko, Calum's scrawny brother. The younger man, barely out of childhood, rocked back and forth. His eyes might have been open, Calum could never tell.

He thought he saw something in there. Under the matted dark tangles, equally dark eyes shone through slitted lids.

Calum decided the kid needed a bath. That meant he'd have to give him one.

"Hey Elko." Calum didn't expect much of a reaction. Elko's rocking slowed, and a sound rose out of him, along with a little line of spittle. He knew the kid was glad to see him. He felt guilty, leaving the kid in the box of a hovel they called home, but somebody needed to make money. "Coins around somewhere?"

A cat—a skinny, boney, patch-haired tabby tom—jumped into Elko's lap. Elko rested his hands on the cat's wasted sides and his rocking slowed. Coins always calmed the kid. It was one of the cat's many gifts.

Calum gave the cat a quick salute. "Not many feasts to gorge yourself on these days, eh Coins?" The cat let out a half-growl, half-meow. "Yeah, well, we need to talk. Elko, is that okay?"

In answer, Elko put his hands on the side of Coins' head. Coins' eyes closed. Elko's opened. They focused on Calum, and one eyebrow rose.

"You shouldn't leave him here with just me around." Elko looked down at the cat, now curled up in his lap. "He feels safe when you're at home. I have to say, I do too."

"I've got a job that may get us out of this hole, Coins," Calum said. "But I'm wondering about it. Thought you might have heard something, maybe through those spirit gossips you listen to."

"There's a lot swirling around right now, my friend." Elko's eyes fixed on Calum's. "There's talk of an imprisoned demon, one of the big ones. This job wouldn't be through the Guild Arcanum, would it?"

"No, it's through one of the local Blackhand bosses," Calum said. "A guy named Josak."

"Josak is rumored to be tongue-to-crack with one of the wizards, though I don't know which." Elko nodded, his gaze unfocused, floating around the room. "This may be for the Arcanum, or maybe a renegade. What's the job?"

Calum wiped his palms on his breeches, suddenly feeling nervous. "Just stealing a jewel, a big one. Reddish, but not a normal jewel."

Elko's eyes re-focused on Calum, his hands resting gently on the cat. "That could be a soul-trap, Tersec."

"Don't call me that," Calum said, scowling. "That name gets out, you know what could happen to me."

Elko looked down at the cat in his lap. "Yes, I can well imagine the consequences of that." Elko sighed, quietly, slumping in the chair. "So, you will still pursue this?"

"Fifty currents." Calum shook his head. "How could I say no to that?"

"You have coin already, yes? Silver perhaps?"

Calum nodded.

"Then we could leave, all of us." Elko's posture improved, his eyes glinting in the weak light of the room. "Let's leave this cesspool of a city, find someplace we can live a quieter life."

"I've never lived anywhere else. Hadrapole is my home. What would I do, farm?"

"There are worse things."

"I'm not a damn farmer, Coins. Maybe I'm not much of anything, but this could make me."

"Or see you dead." Elko's eyes rested on Calum, but Calum offered no response. "You will at least be careful won't you? And not be too gaudy with those tricks I taught you?"

"I'm always careful."

Gently moving the cat aside, Elko rose. He held out an empty hand. "Leave one of your dice."

"What for?" Calum produced one of the dice.

"They'll rattle together," Elko said. "You only need one for luck."

Dropping the purse with the coins on the only table in the hovel, Calum carefully placed one of his bone dice in Elko's hand. He wanted to say more. With Coins there, inhabiting Elko's body, Calum felt like he could talk to his brother, though he knew Elko really existed in the purring tom. Sometimes Calum forgot, and that made remembering all the worse.

He nodded to the purse on the table. "Use some of that silver to get some food for you and the kid."

Calum left before Coins exited Elko's body.

Tanos Six-Toes had few friends, even among the Mashaam. Rumor made him the kind of jackal that gladly feasted on enemy and ally alike. He had stabbed too many backs, so the Mashaam stopped watching his. That didn't mean they would stand for the Blackhands hitting him.

The question that burned in Calum's mind was how Tanos got the jewel.

Stumbling out of the inn, Tanos made crude farewells to his drinking comrades and their feminine entourage. He had no company himself. Calum offered silent thanks to the Heavens for that. He kissed the single dragon die in his left hand, and slid it into the padded pouch at his belt.

Tanos wandered along the street, apparently unworried about traversing the Chain Docks—a notorious part of town— alone. The creaking of wood, the slosh of water and the constant banging of one building striking the next as they all rode the swells made traveling unheard quite easy. The chains and ropes that held Flotsam together groaned as they did each night.

The dark of the streets was almost tangible. Avenues of moonlight reflected off water in the spaces between floating structures but did not reach the walkways, blocked by overhanging eaves and tall, rickety tenements. Calum's eyes, though, cut through the gloom. His hand rested on the short, broad-bladed sword he carried with him. He prayed he wouldn't be called on to use it, but then again, if a whore could cut off four of Tanos' toes, what did Calum have to fear from him?

Turning on to a small side street, even closer and darker than the road he had wandered along, Tanos stopped and turned. Calum shrank back. He had made no noise. Could Tanos feel the eyes on him? Six-Toes glared at the darkness. Surely he couldn't see Calum, who had used his usual tricks to remain unseen.

The pause proved momentary, and soon Tanos moved deeper into the Chain Docks. If anyone could have offered information on where Tanos' lived, Calum could have simply waited in ambush. Still, shadowing Tanos didn't bother him. He wouldn't be spotted. He only wondered about entry into Tanos' room, wherever it was. There would be traps, no doubt, and he would face Tanos on his own terrain.

Tanos again stopped and slowly turned. Calum wondered if maybe Tanos had talents of his own. How could someone that drunk know he was being followed? Calum leaned back, invisible in the shadows. He had another couple of days to get the jewel; further surveillance suddenly appealed to him.

For a moment, it seemed that Tanos had disappeared. Without thinking, Calum moved quickly, though carefully and as silently as possible. Tanos had ducked through a door hidden in a small alcove and now stood in a courtyard, before a particularly shoddy, leaning structure.

Tanos glanced back through the gate and smiled. "I've got tricks of my own, my little shadow, and I'm tempted to use them on you right now."

Before he could follow through on his threat, a figure flew out of an upper story window. It landed, snarling as it did. Roughly man-shaped, it had the hairy snout and the flashing claws of a beast. Under one arm, it cradled a chest. It turned to face Tanos.

29

The beast swung a thick arm, ending in claws. A short, curved sword flashed out from under Tanos' cloak and swept off the beast's arm. He moved far too fast for a drunk man. The beast howled. Dropping the chest, it leaped on Tanos, who now had a second blade out. Calum waited, silent and unmoving, as they rolled on the ground, the beast's jaws snapping, claws raking, Tanos' blades cutting at the beast and driving into it.

Tanos' struggles slowed then ended. The beast rose up. Its fur appeared slick, but in the pale light, Calum couldn't tell if the beast bled or if Tanos' blood covered it. The beast moved toward the chest, lying unattended below the window. It paused and turned. It looked directly at Calum. It growled, baring its teeth.

Apparently, Calum's little talents weren't of much use that night. He had used them, though, and doing so always wore away his inhibitions. He should have fled. Instead, he stepped out of the shadows, dropping the camouflage of darkness.

The chest at the beast's feet surely held the jewel. He knew he had to kill this thing to get it. At that moment, he had some insane assurance in his head that he could actually do that. He risked a glance at Tanos, whose unseeing eyes stared up at the sky. Cuts and bites covered the body. With a growl, the beast charged Calum.

Diving to the side, Calum swung out with his sword. He felt the impact, the sword almost wrenched out of his hand. He recovered his feet. The beast's eyes shone red, a burning behind the pupils. It roared at him, displaying its bloody fangs. It swayed as it stood, its arms held out.

This beast didn't have Flotsam feet. The evening's swell offered Calum an advantage.

He decided to test this thing. With the merest nudge of his talents, he created a distraction—the sound of voices coming from the mouth of the alley. The beast turned, and Calum threw a small, thin knife. The thing moved, but without balance. The blade caught the beast in the temple. It shrieked, plucking out the knife. A slight undulation rolled through the Docks and the thing toppled. Calum thrust with his sword, but the beast knocked it aside. Moving too fast for him to react, the beast grabbed his throat as it regained his feet. Swaying, it lifted him off the ground with its remaining hand.

Calum's vision swam. He feared his neck would snap in the unimaginably powerful grip of the creature. His sword felt slick in his hand, already going numb. With what strength he could muster, he drove the sword up through the creature's jaw, hoping to penetrate whatever brain it might possess. The beast howled. Its grip relaxed. Taking the sword in both hands, Calum stabbed it through one of the beast's eyes. It released his throat.

Landing on his feet, Calum coughed. He stumbled, his legs stubbornly refusing to hold him steadily upright. The beast swung out but its attack lacked the speed and strength exhibited earlier. Calum stayed beyond its reach, taking out another of his throwing knives. Another ripple rolled through the Docks, and the thing stumbled. Calum acted. His throwing knife lodged in the beast's throat. It fell to its knees, clawing at the knife. Calum charged in and slammed his sword through the beast's remaining eye. The creature weakly knocked him away. Calum stumbled, but didn't fall. The beast dropped to the ground, groaning and writhing.

Ignoring both bodies, Calum took the iron chest, small enough to carry in the crook of his arm, and backed away. He fled. He didn't run. A running man aroused suspicion and curiosity. He moved with restrained but purposeful speed through the dark maze of the Chain Docks. He heard the beast still growling and thrashing weakly behind him. The thought flashed through his mind that if the chest didn't hold the jewel, he would need to return to search Tanos' room. The Mashaam would certainly learn of it if he did. And then?

A couple of blocks from the fight, Calum stopped. Feeling the sweat gather on his forehead and armpits, he turned the chest away from him and pried it open with a small crowbar. He didn't apply much force before the lid opened. He froze as the contents became visible in the weak moonlight.

The chest held some scrolls, a pouch with what sounded like coins, and an object wrapped in kerchiefs. He took out that object and unwrapped it. He held in his hand a jewel only slightly smaller than his fist. Very pale red in color, Calum swore it glowed. The light was faint, but it didn't come from the stars or the moon.

Wrapping the jewel up, he thrust it back into the chest and, cradling it under his arm, disappeared into the shadows. Behind him, he could hear shouts and the barking of dogs. Perhaps Tanos and his friend had been found.

Calum slept in his cushioned chair. When he opened his eyes, he saw Coins sitting on Elko's lap and staring at him. Calum rubbed his face and cleared his throat as he sat up. Elko's eyes flickered open, and his mouth twitched. A low grunt, which Calum translated as a good morning, escaped. Coins began to clean himself. Elko didn't start to rock, which Calum took as a good sign.

He didn't bother with a greeting. "I have some stuff for you to hide, Coins."

Coins continued to clean, but he watched Calum as he did.

"I've got to check and find out if I'm going to get gold or a blade for passing this on." Calum tapped the chest with his foot. He had used it as a footrest.

Coins stopped cleaning himself. He meowed. Elko looked down then looked up at Calum.

"If you want to, Elko," Calum said.

Elko made another grunt and placed his hands on the sides of Coins' head. His eyes drifted closed, as did Coins'. Coins curled up in Elko's lap. Elko opened his eyes. He pointed at the chest.

"It's in there, is it?" Elko/Coins asked.

"It is." Calum rubbed his eyes then stretched. "There was something else trying to get it. Something weird. Maybe a demon."

"Then you can bet the Guild Arcanum is involved." Elko scratched behind his ear. "I wonder if perhaps it wouldn't be better to just dump this in the river and disappear."

"There're fifty pieces of minted gold waiting for me."

"That or the end of a knife. You said so yourself."

His bone die found its way into his hand. He rolled it between his fingers. "It's worth the risk. What reason would Josak have for screwing me?"

Elko exhaled slowly. "If it really is Josak and not someone else pulling the strings. Whoever sent the demon may send more, and those things are better hunters than you."

As Calum rose, he heard a few pops from his joints. The previous night had strained him and his talents.

"What else can I do? Have those spirits you commune with told you something?"

"They are silent, which makes me more nervous than when they chatter with dire warnings."

"I'll be careful, Coins." Calum gestured to the chest. "You take care of that."

"Change your clothes. Your tunic is torn and it has black stains all over it."

Calum nodded and slipped off the stained tunic. He tried not to consider the source of the stains. He rooted through his single, small locker, looking for something not stained or torn.

"Tell me something, Coins, you obviously aren't a normal cat, if you are a cat at all." Calum glanced back at Elko, who watched him. "So, why stay a cat? When you found Elko, why didn't you just take his body and go?"

"Because I am a cat," Elko said. "I'm a cat now. What I was before, was before. Besides, there is a certain serenity and tranquility in felinehood. My rational mind wanders while my instincts take over, and then I can contact those you call my 'spirit gossips.' I have learned much since becoming a cat."

Calum took out a tunic with fewer stains and not as worn as the others. "And that's all you'll say?"

Elko ignored the question. "Is that the best tunic you own?"

Calum considered it. "Seems to be, yes."

Elko made a sigil in the air with one hand, twisted the other into an arcane shape and mumbled some words. The stains disappeared and the rips and holes in the tunic mended.

"Could you do that before you were a cat?" Calum asked.

"If we were to leave, find that farm, I could teach you much more than I already have." Elko leaned toward Calum. "There is a wide world out there, full of opportunities that don't rely on cut-throats and sorcerers."

Calum slipped on his tunic. "When I get the gold, we can talk about getting out of Hadrapole. Until then, keep a good eye on the kid. Get those spirit gossips gossiping." Calum pulled open the door. "If I'm not back by tomorrow morning, get the kid out of here."

Calum couldn't decide whether to find Josak or Mandas. Then again, if he went back to the Golden Boar, his favorite haunt, they'd surely find him. Calum moved slowly, staying in crowds, on guard against pickpockets, but trying to remain inconspicuous. He moved near the edge of the crowd, always ready to dart down an alley, or put his back to the wall and haul out a blade.

One didn't dive into the water in Flotsam. Doing so tended to get one crushed between buildings or dragged down to the bottom by the current.

Just before Calum reached the Boar, a hand grasped his shoulder. Spinning, he prepared to defend himself. He froze, mouth hanging open, hand on a dagger hidden at his back. Had he the strength, he would have unintentionally crushed the bone die in his hand. The man standing before him was a slight, bearded man with dark hair. He wore a fashionable tunic and a luxurious fur cloak. He watched Calum through heavy-lidded eyes. Calum recognized the man: Federko, a prominent mage from the Guild Arcanum.

"Do you know me?" Federko asked.

Calum didn't speak; he feared what might come out of his mouth. He nodded. Federko belonged more with the Night Guilds than the Guild Arcanum. He had as much love and compassion as the average sword and was a fair bit deadlier. His vile reputation reached all quarters of Hadrapole.

"Good, then I won't need to threaten you." Federko glanced up the street, to another inn, the Dancing Harlequin. "Let's go to that place, yes? I will follow you."

Calum didn't resist. He didn't consider routes for escape. When touching him, Federko could have placed a marker. If he ran, he'd be found, and he didn't want to consider the consequences of that.

The Harlequin had few in attendance so early in the day. The man behind the bar opened his mouth when Calum walked in, but shut it when Federko followed. Calum sat down at a table near the window. The illusion of an avenue for escape, though he recognized its futility, attracted him.

Federko sat. He stroked his short beard. "I know what you did." He casually gestured toward Calum. "The stink of it clings to you like manure on a farmer. That you killed one of my summoned doesn't bother me, though they come at much expense. That you have the jewel is all that matters. I will pay you well for it."

Calum didn't react.

Federko leaned close, almost comical in his conspiratorial pose. "The jewel is mine. That Tanos fellow stole it from a courier sent to deliver it to me."

Even if Calum believed Federko, he couldn't offer him the jewel, already promised to Josak. If he did, he'd have to run pretty far to escape the Hands. Maybe he couldn't run far enough.

"I know that you are in the hire of Josak, for you see, I hired him." Federko smiled, yellowed, uneven teeth making Calum inwardly cringe. The smile offered no warmth or humor. Did the hawk smile to the rabbit before it tore it to shreds? "I will call him off, give him some of the coin for none of the work and he'll be happy. To you, I can offer two hundred Hadrapole currents for the jewel. Can we agree on that?"

Calum didn't want to say no, even though he knew he should. "If Josak gives me the go ahead, I'll make the deal, but he hired me."

Federko nodded. "Yes, you show discretion and loyalty. Excellent. I will speak with Josak and make an agreement. Do you have the jewel with you?"

Surely he can tell that. Or can he? "No. It's hidden. Somewhere safe."

Federko straightened his cloak as he rose. "I will find you when I need to. Get the jewel and remain somewhere you consider safe."

Federko offered Calum a salute as he left. Calum sat silently, watching him through the slats in the shutters. The crowd parted to let him through.

He's set his seal on me.

Rising on unsteady legs, Calum wondered how far he could run if he started immediately. Coins might have some ideas—he usually did. The Hands, the Guild Arcanum, could Calum dig a deeper grave? He didn't want to consider the result if the Mashaam mistakenly tied him to Tanos' death.

Turning to leave, Calum saw a short, thin man with the sallow face, flat nose and almond shaped eyes approaching him from the shadows at the back of the common room.

Calum profaned all the gods. They just couldn't curse him enough, could they?

Chang the Spear nodded to Calum as he sat down in the chair Federko had recently vacated. Word on the street made Chang out as cold and deadly as any spear. Perhaps that's how he had earned his nickname. Josak, Mandas even Federko had passions, hates and loves. Chang only offered steel-hard carnage. Calum considered running. Maybe he could still find Federko and gain his protection. He dropped that thought immediately. Even Federko had to sleep.

"What do you want with me?" Calum asked.

"I want nothing with you." Eyes still on the crowd, Chang's lips curled slightly. Was that a grin? "I do, however, have a message for you."

Calum considered his options for escape. How far could he get? He couldn't read Chang's expression. Did he expect Calum to run? Did it matter?

Calum glanced around. "What if Federko returns?"

"He won't."

"What if someone here talks of us meeting?"

"They won't" Chang's eyes wandered through the crowd. "I saw your discussion with Federko."

Well, at least he's honest. "I don't suppose you could hear what we were talking about."

Chang pointed at Calum's face. "I could tell what you said by watching your lips. We suspected you had the jewel, now we know."

"We?" The use of the plural worried Calum.

"I have an employer also."

"But you aren't with either Night Guild."

Chang clasped his hands in his lap. "That is correct, however I do have an employer. My employer does not wish anyone else to obtain the jewel. It is very dangerous."

"Federko said it was his jewel."

"He lied. The courier was bringing the jewel to my employer when Tanos stole it."

Calum shrugged. "I've been hired for a job, Chang. What can I do?"

Chang reached beneath the thin, wool coat he wore and pulled out a small slip of white paper. Calum's eyes narrowed. Only the richest of the Hadrapole rich used paper. He had only seen a sheet of it once. Chang handed the paper to Calum.

"My employer wishes to illustrate the goodwill he bears you," Chang said. "He has told me that on this paper is something that will show he could take what he wants. He would rather negotiate and obtain another ally."

Calum looked down at the paper. The two words on it were written in ancient Saddunen ideograms, a script commonly used by wizards and sorcerers. The ideograms read 'Tersec Vries.' Chang's employer had Calum's true name. He could have easily stripped Calum of all his tricks and talents, and then fed his soul to the demon in the jewel. He still could. Did Calum dare trust this unnamed benefactor?

Chang gestured to the paper. "I have been told that you are a wizard."

"Not much of one."

"Not now, but with training, who can say?"

Chang watched Calum, no emotion penetrating his mask of a face. On the street, Chang's reputation was fearsome, but he was said to be an honest man. If any honor remained among thieves, it resided with this small, dangerous man. A man like that would not fit in well with the Hands or the Mashaam, which may have been the reason they let him remain the wildcard in an otherwise ordered chaos.

"You're persuasive," Calum said. "I have one question."

Chang raised one finger. "I know the question you will ask. I am allowed to answer it. My employer is Philitos, the Urban Tribune."

Leaning back in his chair, his limbs feeling like lead, Calum swallowed and closed his eyes. Philitos, the man who policed Hadrapole, the enemy of the Hands and the Mashaam. Chang was his man? In a strange, perverse way, it made sense. Who else but the most dangerous man, respected and feared by all the criminals of the city, would escape suspicion as an informant and enforcer of the law?

"He is a man of honor, a man of his word." Chang's voice made Calum open his eyes. "You do not need to fear him. He will not allow you to pass the jewel on, but he bears you no ill-will."

Calum rubbed his cheek. The Urban Tribune wanted him? Sure, he had abilities and talents that Philitos might find useful, but he wasn't knife-edge deadly like Chang.

"We know about your brother," Chang said. "We are sympathetic. No man who puts his life in jeopardy to support his family can be an altogether evil man. I am also to remind you that an alliance with the Urban Tribune can prove profitable to you. I have not been adversely affected by my relationship with Philitos."

"But you're you." Calum waved his hand at Chang. "You're the Spear. Nobody would cross you."

"I know that you are uncertain about accepting this offer because you feel some loyalty to the criminal element with whom you have worked. I ask you, though, if they could profit from your demise, would they pause before driving the knife through your heart?"

Calum almost laughed. "You and I both know they'd go to it with a smile on their face, any of them."

Chang nodded. "Your loyalty is misplaced. The very fact that you have such loyalty separates you from the others. Philitos can offer safety and stability for your family, and honorable work for you."

"Listen, Josak goes missing then I disappear, or show up with gold in my purse, the Hands are going to point the finger at me. I won't last long."

"Federko has told the Guild Arcanam nothing of the jewel and Josak has not informed the Hands about his relationship with Federko. No one but Federko and Philitos knows that Josak has hired you. The Hands will not become involved, and neither will the Guild Arcanum. Their secrecy and manipulations now work in your favor."

"The Grunt knows."

Chang's brow furrowed. He frowned. "By the Grunt I assume you mean Mandas?"

Calum nodded.

"It is our belief that Federko intends to kill Josak rather than pay him. I would assume Mandas will meet the same fate." Chang scratched his cheek. "If not, I will secure their silence."

Calum didn't want to consider the implications of securing silence. "If I agree to this, what do I do?"

Calum swore that a genuine, warm smile spread across Chang's face. It disappeared the moment Chang began to speak. "You return home, gather your family and what belongings you cherish, and go to the Red Jester. It is safe. The innkeeper knows to expect you."

"Do I meet Philitos?"

"Do you wish to?"

Calum didn't want to say what he thought. He paused.

Chang opened his arms, showing his palms. "Say what you wish."

"I don't know if I completely trust you."

Chang nodded. "A wise decision. Philitos will meet you, and you may present the jewel to him in person."

Calum inhaled deeply. "I'll think about it. Give me a day. I'll meet you back here."

Chang didn't react. Having said what he had to, Calum rose from the chair and left. With each step, he half-expected to die with a sword in his gut. He made it out the door unscathed.

The sun had set by the time Calum arrived home. He had covered almost all the Chain Docks, walking, lost in thoughts and worries. His lone bone die rolled in his hand. He had accepted Chang's story too easily. Maybe because he wanted to. The hope of escaping from Josak and Federko, of doing what was right for once, was perhaps too strong. Why else would he have accepted Chang's explanation so quickly?

Well, he had trusted Mandas when he had offered the job. He had believed Federko when he had said he would pay off Josak and then offer more gold for the jewel. The day had just been one for trust. And among the three, only Chang had a good reputation. By the time Calum reached his home, he knew what he had to do. If not for himself, for Elko.

His lack of focus left him vulnerable. His hand rested on the door to his hovel-home when something solid connected just below his skull, on his neck. He fell forward, hitting the door, then turning as he sank to the ground. The die rolled out of his hand. The blow had hurt, but he always wore protective spells. He acted much more stunned than he felt.

Mandas stood there with three thugs. Calum guessed they were Hands. Mandas held a thick club, its head covered in iron. Without his spells, Calum knew he would be unconscious, if not dead.

"What did you do to Josak?" Mandas asked.

Had Federko killed Josak or had Chang? Did it matter? Calum squirmed on the ground, trying to buy time, hoping Mandas cared more about answers than hurting him. Mandas leaned down, brandishing his club.

"Come on, Calum, where's Josak?"

"Federko" Calum slurred his speech slightly, offering it up slowly, trying to give the impression of a man barely aware.

"The wizard?"

Oh yeah, you are the bright one. "Federko's after Josak. I'm next."

"Why?"

Now I know the real reason they call you Grunt.

Calum swallowed, clutching the back of his neck, squinting. He hoped he looked weak, nonthreatening. "He's the one who hired Josak. Now that Josak's gone, he'll be coming for me."

Mandas paused. He looked at the other three thugs, murmuring amongst themselves. Calum could read the uncertainty on his face. This one didn't usually make decisions. Options stymied this boot-lick. If Calum could keep him like that, keep him from acting, he might walk out of this.

A scream tore through the pale light of the early evening. Mandas spun. Two of his thugs threw themselves back, yelling and reaching for weapons. The third wrestled with a wiry, hairy creature. The thing had one muscular arm and one scrawny one, both ending in claws. Scars rent its fur in many places. Calum sent up a silent curse.

The beast from Tanos' tenement still lived. Federko had offered him more than one lie.

The thug put up less of a struggle than Tanos had. The creature bore him to the ground and ripped out his throat. It howled, half-way between a yell and gurgle. Mandas surprised Calum by taking a swing at the creature. The thing blocked the club with its good arm and leaped on Mandas. The other two thugs fled, crying out supplications to a dozen different gods.

Calum began to concentrate. He didn't have many spells of power, nothing that might slow the creature, but any distraction could give Calum the chance to get past it. He had to draw the creature away from his home. If Federko discovered where Calum lived, he surely wouldn't pause at torturing Elko to find the location of the jewel. Even if this thing killed him, Calum trusted in Coins to get Elko out of the city using the money already accumulated.

He should have moved then, ran while the thing tore into Mandas. He didn't. Calling on his magic always lowered his inhibitions. It was the price he paid for that small power. With each stretch of his talents, his rational mind lost ground. Rather than run, he sat and watched as the creature finished with Mandas. The thug's body lay in three large sections in a growing pond of dark blood. Calum had his sword out, the same sword he had driven into the creature's head. What good would it do? The beast turned to Calum, its empty eye sockets emitting a pale red light.

Before Calum could act, a streak of steel flashed from above and the creature stumbled back. A long, thin dirk, almost the length of a sword, stuck out of its head. Chang dropped from a rooftop, a sword swinging out, severing the creature's muscular arm. Chang landed, back to Calum, sword ready.

"You have made enemies," Chang said. "You are lucky I was watching."

The beast staggered to the left then the right. Calum had not noticed the tidal swells, but that thing had no legs for it. Chang moved in. The beast tried to fend him off, but with each swing of Chang's sword, a little more of the beast spattered the walls.

Calum had his doubts that even Chang could kill that thing. He should have run while Chang distracted the thing. He should have led both it and Chang away from his family. He didn't. He had spells of protection woven like armor and he readied a charm of distraction. The use of his magic had removed his reticence. Getting to his feet, he faced the beast with the calm, insane conviction of a drunk. If he was going to die, he'd do it fighting. He noticed the mist forming at Chang's feet, but it didn't really register. He took a hesitant step forward, then the relevance of the mist struck him.

"Chang—" He had no chance to complete his warning.

A crackling finger of lightning lanced down and struck Chang. It threw him to the side. He lay there, arm hanging over the edge of a walkway, fingers licked by the waves. Smoke rose from him. Calum could not tell if he lived.

Federko stood just behind the beast, resting his hand on the creature's scarred head.

"It seems this is a dangerous world for men like you, Master Calum."

Calum couldn't find any words. He actually felt moisture forming in his eyes. A tight rock of frustration weighed down his guts.

"You have the jewel, yes?" Federko held out his hand, as though Calum would pass the jewel to him there.

"Not here." Calum's voice came as a bare croak.

"Is this your home?" Federko looked over the small hovel. He shook his head. "I would have expected something better. Perhaps you can find a nicer home after I've paid you."

Calum's head had not yet cleared. The back of his neck still throbbed. It wouldn't slow him. He wondered if he could reach Federko before the beast could intervene. "You're not going to pay me. I know that."

Federko smiled. "The hope of it was enough, though, to bring you to this. It's funny, even at the very end Josak thought he would receive his coin." Federko exhaled loudly, almost a sigh. "No matter. Give me the jewel and I won't kill you."

Calum allowed a sneer to grow on his lips—pure bravado. "Yes you will. No matter what I do, I'm dead."

Federko's smile faded. "You can die quickly or slowly. And there are many places for your soul to travel."

With discrete movement, Calum had his hand on his throwing knife. One through Federko's eye, and Calum would take his chances with the beast. He sent up a silent prayer to any god who might listen to preserve Elko and Coins.

The door behind Calum creaked open. Federko retreated behind the beast. Calum kept the knife in his hand. Out of the door stepped Elko, but Calum realized it couldn't be Elko; this person stood too straight, the eyes appeared too lucid, the mouth set in determination.

"If I had known I'd be seeing you, Federko, I would have been sure to invite all the demons in the Twelve Hells." The voice came from Elko's mouth, but Calum knew Coins spoke. Elko shook Calum's other dragon bone die in his right hand.

Federko's eyes narrowed. "I don't know you."

Elko took another step, bringing him to stand beside Calum. "Oh, you don't know this body, but do you remember Addin of Lest?"

Federko's eyes widened, his jaw fell, and he pointed with a shaking hand. "I banished your soul after I named your true name. Addin of Lest is dead. "

"He most certainly is." Elko chuckled. He pointed to the beast, which growled and hissed. "Is this your toy?"

Words in the language of a civilization that had died a thousand years previous came from Elko's mouth. Calum knew that language, and its potency in casting. The beast had time to almost reach Elko, barely an arm's length away. Elko's hand shot forward in a blur of motion. The die struck the creature in the forehead. Both dissolved into dust. Calum saw no flash, heard no sound. One moment the beast's claws reached for Elko, the next moment a cloud of dust slowly settled to the ground.

Federko had a small fetish—a finger sized doll, wrapped in something which could have been hair, tying a shard of metal to it—in his hand as he spoke words in the same arcane language. He finished his incantation and gestured at Elko.

"I name you by your true name and bind your power, Hoshin Qay." Federko waved the fetish at Elko. "I bind you to me, Hoshin Qay. Submit."

The air thickened with tension. Calum found breathing difficult. He still held his knife behind his back, his short fighting sword in his right hand. He glanced at Elko, unsure of what to expect. To Calum's surprise, Elko smiled. A chuckle rippled out of him, bordered with disdain.

"That worked once, but this body isn't Hoshin Qay's," Elko said.

Federko took a step back. He dropped the fetish. "If you think to meet me strength for strength, you will find that I've improved, and learned much."

Elko leaned forward, as though bracing himself. Sparks and energy cascaded off both Elko and Federko. Calum had never seen a spell-battle before. Both men stood rooted to the ground, chanting in low voices, their hands drawing obscure symbols in the air, their eyes locked. Calum knew that a duel of spells might lead to Elko's death, or at least the death of Elko's body. That would mean an end to Coins and Elko trapped as a cat.

Elko grunted and dropped to one knee. Federko began to smile. That goaded Calum into action. He charged, sword ready. He couldn't risk a glance at Elko. He swung his sword, praying Elko's magic would drain Federko enough to leave him vulnerable. The sword glanced off the air a hand's span from Federko, raising sparks.

Calum screamed in frustration, battering a Federko, never reaching him. He stepped back, panting. Chang groaned. Calum glanced at him. He saw Chang held a thin dagger in one hand. Silver etchings covered the black blade. Calum recognized the etchings as Saddunen ideograms.

Calum grabbed the dagger from Chang's weak grip. He turned. Elko was on his knees, one hand supporting him, the other reaching out. Federko's chant had increased in speed and volume. Calum lunged at Federko.

The dagger sliced across Federko's throat. A gurgle replaced the chant issuing from his mouth. Calum drove the dagger deep into Federko's shoulder. The wizard stumbled forward, one arm hanging useless at his side, his other hand clutching at his throat. Red and green flames danced around his body, though leaving no burns or marks. Calum stabbed at Federko's head, the dagger a blur of motion. Federko fell to the ground, but Calum didn't stop.

A hand on his shoulder made Calum spin. He raised the dagger to strike, then let it fall to his side. Elko smiled at him.

"You're very fast."

Calum released the breath he had been holding. "Desperation helps." He dropped the dagger to the ground. "You *are* Coins, right?"

Elko shrugged. "Coins, Addin of Lest, Hoshin Qay, I've had many names."

Calum looked over at Federko. Blood poured from his many head wounds, but he continued to crawl away. Chang still lay where he fell, but Calum knew he lived.

"We need to help Chang," Calum said.

"You do," Elko replied. "He cannot know I live. A secret shared is no secret at all."

Calum nodded. He considered Federko. "Would he have killed you?"

Elko raised an eyebrow. "What would you think?"

Calum shook his head. "I don't know. It looked as though he was going to beat you."

"I'm not the wizard I was when Federko learned my true name." Elko stooped down and came up with an object in his hand. He tossed it to Calum. "You must have dropped that. You only need one for luck."

Calum caught the dragon bone die. He rattled it in his hand as he watched Federko struggle to escape. "How do we deal with him?"

Elko frowned and advanced on the weakly struggling form. "I'll take care of him. You see to Chang."

Calum sat across from Chang at the Red Jester. It felt strange to stand on solid ground. He had no balance. Even on the calmest of days, Flotsam moved. Hadrapole did not.

He twirled his die on the table. Coins purred contentedly in his lap, having consumed a fair portion of Calum's stew. Elko was already safely ensconced in a private room. Coins' use of the body seemed to have exhausted him. A short, balding man in tunic and breeches under an Imperial robe sat at the same table. Philitos, the Urban Tribune, rested his hands on the small chest that held the jewel.

"I'm afraid Federko has eluded our grasp," Philitos said. "Perhaps some time with the garrison might be in your best interest."

Calum let out a quiet snort of amusement. "Don't worry about Federko."

Chang nodded. "You are a man of hidden talents if you could defeat Federko."

"Wizards don't die so easily," Philitos said. "Maybe you should direct us to the body. We'll dispose of it in the proper manner."

Calum took out a large pouch that hung under his arm and dropped it on the table. Some ash rose from its mouth. "I've seen to that."

Philitos nodded. Rising, he took the pouch. "I'll contact you through Chang when I need you. Your fifty currents are in the innkeeper's strongbox. Whenever you wish, Chang will take you to your quarters in Twelve-Shadow Walk."

Calum's eyes grew wide. "Twelve-Shadow Walk? Well, I guess we are moving up in the world."

"You'll find working with me is much more profitable than working against me." Philitos hefted the pouch in his hand, as though weighing it. "I have to ask; how did you kill a wizard as powerful as Federko?"

"I can answer that if you can tell me how you found my true name." Calum snatched up his die.

Philitos' eyes narrowed. He frowned. "I have my ways."

Calum leaned back in his chair, stroking Coins, "As do I."

- the end -

For Simple Coin

Victories don't come much sweeter than this. The premier Canadian speculative fiction journal, *On Spec*, not only bought "For Simple Coin," I was the featured author for their Winter 2009 issue and got an interview along with my story. The story I can bring you, given that it's mine. If you want to read the interview, you'll need to get a back issue.

I can share with you the crux of the interview, and that's my philosophy on writing. I'm a hack.

Let me explain. I know I am no genius. I am not Joseph Conrad. I am not Fritz Leiber. I am not Guy Gavriel Kay. My writing is not going to change speculative fiction. I will never write the great Canadian novel. I don't delude myself. I believe I am a competent writer, and given that professional publications are willing to pay me for my work, I have some evidence for that. I believe that I can write an entertaining story, and there is also evidence to back this up. But I sell my work, I don't give it away. I do this for the love of writing, but if you want my story, you'll need to pay for it.

The image of the impoverished writer suffering for his art is certainly romantic, but I've never been one enamoured of suffering, expect on the written page—there's drama in suffering but I prefer comfort, thank you very much. When I write, I'm generally looking for a pay cheque. I don't want "exposure," I don't need "visibility"—if the publisher is getting paid and the writer isn't, I call bullshit.

That's not to say that I wouldn't write without the mercenary motivation of money. I love writing. I'm also not saying that I never give stuff away. Check out swordedgepublishing.ca and swordsedge.ca for free stuff. You see, if I'm going to give something away, I want to do it in a way that might actually accrue some attention to me.

I'm a writer, I can't help but write. When I started out, before I learned how the business worked—and it is, indeed, a business—I did give a couple of stories away for free. Thing is, the places that got those stories also didn't make any money, so really no harm no foul. These days I stay far, far away from venues that expect readers to pay, but want me to give them my stories for little or no money.

So I'm a hack. I write for profit, yes. I write things I plan to sell. But I still have the impulse to write. I think there are very, very few people who can write only for money, who don't also do it for love. Think of us like directors or producers of movies and television—we love what we do, but we do it for money.

And that was the crux of the interview. It's title? "Mercenary Hack of the Fantasy World." I love that title.

FOR SIMPLE COIN

The crowd on the street flowed, not slowing, ignorant of the peril Caspan Trey could all but taste. His eyes fixed on his home, a shack built on the side of a warehouse used by smugglers. The door to the hovel he called home hung open. He considered his options, knowing he had only two—enter his home or leave Elnya to her fate. He had promised to protect her. Had given his word.

Caspan drew his sword, careful to keep it beneath his cloak. Feeling leather wrapped over cold steel in his hand helped him concentrate. Elnya had feared the Witch-Finders. Had they found her? Could they still be in the hovel?

Though he made no conscious decision, Caspan started toward his home. He noted a break in the mass of people. Two men surged out from the crowd. Each carried a short sword.

Caspan swore under his breath and spun. A throwing dagger flew from his off-hand. One man grunted and fell, the knife buried up to the hilt in his shoulder. The second man paused. Caspan did not. In two steps, he was within reach and swinging. The man's parry was clumsy. Caspan kicked the clumsy man's shins. Clumsy stumbled back and Caspan sliced open his throat. As Clumsy crumpled, his hand at his neck, Caspan advanced on the wounded man.

Their complete lack of professionalism angered Caspan. Did they not know who he was, what he was? "Who sent you?"

The bleeding man said nothing. Bleeder began to crawl away. Caspan put his boot on the dagger hilt. Bleeder cried out.

Caspan leaned close. "Who sent you?"

Bleeder grabbed Caspan's leg. With a quick turn and surprising strength, he knocked Caspan to the ground. Bleeder scrambled over to him, a long, curved dagger in his hand. The pommel of Caspan's sword cracked against Bleeder's temple, felling him. Caspan rose quickly, snatching up the curved dagger. The blood from Bleeder's forehead mixed with that flowing from his shoulder.

Caspan placed his sword's blade against Bleeder's throat. "Who sent you?"

Mumbling something, Bleeder grabbed for Caspan. The sword's blade slid along his neck. Caspan cursed. Bleeder gurgled as the blood foamed out of his mouth and drained from his neck to the road.

Retrieving his dagger and stepping back, Caspan surveyed the crowd. They watched with little interest and no passion. Two men lay in rapidly expanding pools of their own blood and no one in the crowd moved to assist.

Leaving the bodies, Caspan burst into his empty room through the door, which hung loose on its rope hinges. His single chair lay on the ground, but otherwise Caspan saw no sign of a struggle. Had the Witch-Finders taken her? Could their agents be fanatical enough to die rather than talk?

Caspan would find answers in only one place.

Through the darkening streets of Hadrapole, Caspan moved with cautious speed. Every individual had a knife destined for his heart. Every glance came from an agent of the Witch-Finders. His heart beat and his palms sweat. The cool night air made him think of metal against his skin.

What little he knew he had learned from Terqmar at the Singing Swan. The Witch-Finders came from the Kingdoms to hunt sorcerers. That would not help him find Elnya. He intended to learn more.

Caspan paused as he came within sight of the Swan, the crowd so thick he couldn't tell if he'd been followed. It didn't matter. He had killed two and would kill again if needed.

The Swan held fewer patrons than he had expected. To Caspan's relief, Terqmar sat on his regular stool at the end of the bar. He had spoken of the Witch-Finders with the blind man earlier that day. Terqmar also knew of secret ways to enter the city walls, and he had contacts with the Mashaam, one of the city's two Night Guilds.

Terqmar sat silently, his filmy eyes staring straight ahead, unseeing. One hand rested on a tin plate which held some bones and the remains of what may have been a meal. In his other, he held a tankard. His patched, worn clothes—tunic and breeches with the robes of a desert nomad overtop—hung loose about his scant frame. His dark hair peeked out from beneath a discoloured, dingy turban. His angular, clean-shaven face sported many creases and lines for a man who otherwise didn't look much more than four decades old.

Terqmar turned to face him almost as soon as Caspan's eyes rested on him. "I had not expected to see you again so soon, Caspan Trey."

Taking the seat next to Terqmar, Caspan waved the barkeep over and ordered a jug of brandy and two cups. The barkeep didn't move until Caspan slapped down a copper *as*.

"Very kind of you." Terqmar leaned close and dropped his voice to a whisper. "But you have not come to drink to success, rather you seek an ally against the Witch-Finders, yes?"

The uncanny knowledge Terqmar displayed had originally frightened Caspan. He didn't understand magic and tried to steer clear of wizards. Experience had taught him that Terqmar posed no threat, and so the blind man became just another of Hadrapole's unexplained curiosities. Caspan waited until the brandy and cups arrived and the barkeep moved out of earshot. No one sat near enough to overhear the two.

"When the Witch-Finders capture someone, where do they take them?"

Terqmar raised his hand. "Are we not getting somewhat ahead of ourselves? No pleasantries, no discussion of payment?"

"I've just killed two men, Terqmar," Caspan said. "I believe they were agents of the Witch-Finders."

"But not Witch-Finders themselves?" Terqmar tapped his chin with a single finger. "Why not Witch-Finders?"

"I killed them too easily."

"You are brighter than many imagine. I would surmise you have lost your patron. Who is she?"

"Then you don't know? But you know she's a woman?"

"You have something of the romantic in you," Terqmar said. "You feel protective of women and children in a way you do not feel towards men, even your friends." The thin shadow of a wary grin danced at the corners of Terqmar's mouth. "And besides, I smelled her upon you when we spoke earlier. Who is she?"

"Her name is Elnya. She sells charms and curses out of the Old Bazaar near the Lampwright's Walk."

Terqmar nodded. "I know of her. She is a kind young lady, touched only slightly with the talent. I am surprised the Witch-Finders would have interest in her."

"Do they have interest in you?"

Terqmar patted Caspan's clenched fist. "I have a benefactor who protects me."

"Would this benefactor . . . ?" Caspan feared asking the question, feared its answer.

One of Terqmar's eyebrows arched. "Do we have the time it would take me to find him, contact him and await his answer?"

"No." The answer came from Caspan as a growl. "So tell me, you seem to know everything; where did they take her?"

"While I thank you for the compliment, I assure you I do not know everything. However, if you have a thing of hers, perhaps I could find her, if they have not taken her far."

Caspan shoved the purse of coins Elnya had paid him at Terqmar. "Her silver . . ."

"Will not do." Terqmar pushed the purse back into Caspan's hand. "It is not personal enough. I need something of hers, not something she has merely held."

"I know where she sold her charms, in the bazaar, but I don't know where she slept," Caspan said.

"Take me to her place in the bazaar. I will find what I need there."

Caspan rose off his stool. Terqmar put a restraining hand on his arm. "Tell me, will you attempt to rescue her if we find where they hold her?"

Caspan hesitated for a moment. "I will."

"Who is this Elnya the Charm-seller whose hold over you is so strong that you would risk your life flagrantly and willingly?"

"I'm paid to risk my life and to take others. I don't think much about it."

"This is not about coins and oaths," Terqmar said. "What power does she have over you?"

Caspan cast about in his mind for an answer. He only found one. "She's beautiful."

"Perhaps you are not as clever as I thought." Terqmar laughed quietly. "Let us go to where she held court in the bazaar and I will see if I can find what I need."

Terqmar sprang off his stool. He picked up a cane with an elaborate metal head and started toward the door. Caspan inhaled deeply and set off after him. Those few people in the tavern leaned away from Terqmar, watching him with a mixture of suspicion and fear. They considered Caspan with mild curiosity but little else.

On the streets, Terqmar moved with assurance and grace, his stride purposeful and long. He used the metal-headed walking stick, his cane, more as an affectation than as a prop or a tool. Caspan followed close behind, wondering at the skills of this supposedly blind man.

The Lampwright's Walk and the Old Bazaar lay near the Gates of Empire. The gong marking the city's closing had sounded soon after sunset. Terqmar halted in the shadow of a tenement on the Walk. He seemed to scan his surroundings, his head turning as though casting his gaze over the wide street. Caspan swore he heard him sniff. Light spread out from the handful of taverns and other establishments still entertaining guests. A few pedestrians traversed the Walk, most of them stumbling, calling to each other in drunken slurs.

Terqmar straightened. "You have a reputation as being rather accomplished with your blades. Is it warranted?"

"I'd say it is."

"That is good." Terqmar pointed down the walk with his cane. "Something was there, may still be there, likely the Witch-Finders. The stink of it masks any other sign I might read."

"You think they're waiting for us?" Caspan slid his sword a hand's-span out of its scabbard.

"They found her in your hovel, did they not? They might guess you would follow. Why else leave the two assassins?"

Caspan drew his sword, hidden beneath his cloak. "I'll see if there's a trap or ambush to worry about."

"Lead on, then, but I will be close behind. You may need my help."

Caspan's eyebrows rose. "I appreciate the offer, but aren't you blind?"

"Am I?"

Caspan shook his head with exasperation. "I honestly don't know. If this is bravado, it's misplaced. "

"In the darkness, I perceive much better than you." Terqmar started down the street, his cane swinging at his side.

The two moved down the side of the road, avoiding its center, watching the rooftops and the side-streets. Terqmar had spoken true. While Caspan occasionally stumbled over an unseen rut or rock in the road, Terqmar moved with an assured step. They reached the square called the Old Bazaar, where merchants held the daily market. Nothing moved in the square that night.

"She usually has her wares on a rug..." Caspan had no opportunity to finish.

"And her home is right here." Terqmar pointed to a door in the tenement behind the place Elnya sold her charms and trinkets.

Caution forgotten, Caspan rushed across the square, intent on flinging open the door, be damned any waiting assassins. He reached for the door, but something held him. He would not call it dread, perhaps unease but nothing more than that. Still, it made him pause, did not allow him to actually touch the door.

"They did not come here," Terqmar swept past Caspan and stood with his face a fraction of a finger from the door. "There are sigils on this portal, all but hidden. They have power behind them, more than our little charm-seller ever displayed."

Terqmar scratched at the wood with the head of his cane. Caspan almost lunged forward, the compulsion that had held him at bay gone.

"Sigils, though, work on the eyes, even when one does not know one has seen them." Terqmar tapped his cheek just below his right eye. "Not appropriate for keeping me away."

Pushing open the door, Terqmar entered. Caspan did not. He wasn't even certain he wanted to see Elnya's home. He wanted her to remain, in some ways, a secret to him. He wanted to preserve the tangible pleasure he received from the unknown that hung about her like a subtle perfume. He wondered at his own reaction. Inside that room could lay the clue that would lead him to Elnya, that might help him save her. Why did he hesitate?

Terqmar stood just inside the room, a charm on a worn, dark-leather loop in his hand. "I believe I have found your young charge's protection. This and the sigils on the door are known to me. They are marks of my own benefactor."

58

"Your benefactor? Who?"

"Is it important?" Terqmar asked. "Our shared benefactor could not protect her. Our time is drawing short. In this place, infused with Elnya's essence, I can see clearly the danger she is in."

Caspan grabbed Terqmar's shoulders. "What is it? Where is she?"

Terqmar put a hand on Caspan's arm. "They have her not far from here, but inside the walls of Hadrapole. I know what they want from her. They want her blood."

"What?" Caspan pulled away from Terqmar, taking two strides back into the square. "Are you going to tell me we fight vampires?"

"No, much worse." Terqmar stepped out of the room. "She has power in her and they hope to take that power from her by taking that which gives her life. They will exsanguinate her and use her blood in ceremonies intended to lead them to our sanctuary, to my benefactor."

"I didn't think they were wizards."

"They are not, but they have magic," Terqmar said. "This they can do. She is tied to my benefactor, as am I. They will be able to strike at him through her, through her blood."

"Then we need to get inside Hadrapole."

Terqmar started off, moving north. "And we will. The Gates of the Empire are open to us this night." Terqmar pointed to the sky with his cane. "It is the Moonless Hour, the time of blindness."

"Does that help a blind man?"

"Did I say I was a blind man?" Terqmar smiled. "I am a sightless man. It does not necessarily follow that I am blind." He moved away with a sure step

Caspan rushed after him, and they soon reached the Imperial Highway. The activity on it consisted mostly of people traversing across, rather than along it. Few traveled east, leaving the city on the route that would lead to the Empire. None traveled west, which lead to the closed gates. No soldiers guarded the gates. Who could force them open without an army and siege engines?

"At the proper time, we will enter the near pedestrian gate." Terqmar pointed at the iron-banded door, shielded by a closed portcullis.

"And at that time the portcullis will be raised?"

"As I said, at the proper time, we will enter the near pedestrian gate." Terqmar leaned back against the building in whose shadow they stood. "What will you do when you face these Witch-Finders?"

"I'll find out if good steel wins against foul magic," Caspan said.

"So simple, is it?"

"If you have some other idea—"

Terqmar raised his hand and Caspan paused. "The magic of the Witch-Finders is not particularly impressive, and I have no doubt that your steel would win against one, or perhaps two. And if we face more than two?"

"Do you carry weapons?"

Terqmar opened his mouth as though to answer, but then he frowned. He grabbed Caspan's tunic. "The time is now."

Caspan followed Terqmar along the building, then across the Imperial Walk to the pedestrian gate. The portcullis remained in place. Caspan let out an annoyed sigh. He opened his mouth to speak, to curse, but he did neither.

Terqmar walked through the portcullis and the door.

Caspan stood before the portal, staring. A blind man filling a cup without spilling a drop, Caspan could accept. It stretched the bounds of normal for him, but he could accept it. Walking through a portcullis and a door as though through an insubstantial mist, he could not accept. Was Terqmar a ghost, some spirit visible only to Caspan?

"Come along." Terqmar's voice came from beyond the door. "If you want to save that pretty charm-seller, follow me."

When Caspan reached out to test the portcullis, his hand drifted through it and the door. Though his eyes saw them, his hand touched nothing. He stepped forward and through the unresisting, immaterial barriers. Beyond those barriers now, in the tunnel of the pedestrian gate, Caspan turned to see nothing. The door slowly creaked closed as the portcullis slid down.

"A simple illusion," Terqmar said. "If that gives you pause, how will you fare against these Witch-Finders?"

Not offering a reply, Caspan pushed past Terqmar. He had asked himself the same question all through the night. What would he do when he faced magic—real magic? He would strike fast and hard, he would fight dirty and offer no quarter. What else could he do?

Caspan advanced through the portal, exiting through a door and portcullis as insubstantial and illusory as the last. Caspan watched as Terqmar stepped out of the wood and iron.

"Where now?" asked Caspan.

Setting off down a side-street leading south, Terqmar gestured for Caspan to follow. Caspan knew nothing of the streets of Hadrapole proper. He had never had business inside the walls, nor the kind of coin entertainment in the city demanded. Every step he took increased the tightness in his chest. His heart demanded release, and his hands could not promise to remain steady. A moment's hesitation and Caspan felt certain his legs would give way.

Terqmar stopped. He put a hand over his face and groaned. Caspan rushed to him.

"What is it?" Caspan asked.

"We are here." Terqmar pointed to a tall wall.

Caspan couldn't swallow. He held his sword in a moist hand. He considered the wall, then Terqmar who appeared to have recovered.

"What was wrong?" Caspan asked.

"I believe our time is running out. There are four Witch-Finders and they have your charm-seller. They perform some ceremony or rite, preparing to spill her blood. They're gathered near the rear of the building."

"We go over?" Caspan put his hand on the wall.

Terqmar crossed his arms, still holding his cane. "How?"

Caspan looked around. The side-street was empty of anything large or sturdy enough to stack against the wall. He sheathed his sword. "You boost me up, then I'll pull you over."

"Is that so?"

"Is this such a bad plan?"

Terqmar grimaced. "I suppose it could be worse." Leaning his cane against the wall, he cupped his hands before him. "Over you go."

Caspan had not expected Terqmar's strength. He climbed from Terqmar's steady cupped hands to his sturdy shoulders and then the top of the wall. He surveyed the grounds. The illumination from the street did not pass the walls, but Caspan could make out trees, shrubs, a small building, and shadows. Steadying himself, he reached down and grasped Terqmar's hands. Terqmar proved quite agile, quickly scaling the wall while still holding his cane in one hand.

The two lay on the wall, staring into the compound. Caspan considered the building, a single story, its windows shuttered, no light escaping. The door faced a small walk, which led to a gate in the front wall. In through the door or one of the windows? And then how long until he lay dead?

Caspan heard Terqmar grunt, and saw him holding a hand in front of his eyes.

"I cannot see," Terqmar said.

"Of course you can't see."

"No, you do not understand." Terqmar reached for Caspan but missed. He waved his hand until he caught hold of Caspan's cloak. "I have spells and ensorcellments that allow me to sense the world around me much better than a man with eyes. Something has happened and those spells are gone. I am now as people have always thought. I cannot see. I cannot help you."

Eyes wide, staring at the sightless man now truly blind, Caspan froze. What now? He faced the Witch-Finders alone, without even the help of a blind man. Who was he to confront a group of wizards, or whatever they were? What prize did he seek?

No prize, simply a woman's life. An innocent woman he thought he might love. "I can continue from here. You've done more than I could ever repay."

"I have a purpose here, Caspan Trey. These Witch-Finders threaten me and mine. You are here for simple coin and maybe lust. Neither is worth your life. You do not need to go forward."

"Yes, my friend, I do."

Terqmar released Caspan.

"My prayers go with you, my friend."

"I'll be back for you when I am done."

Caspan slid from the wall, landing with a dull thud on the soft turf of the lawn. He crept to the nearest window, and took a few deep, steadying breaths. Four men, not expecting him, were inside intent on whatever cruelty they practiced on Elnya. He had his sword, his speed and his experience. They had magic.

He held out his hand to touch the shutter, and test its strength. He couldn't. An unaccustomed sensation sped through him. Fear. The longer he waited, the more it would weaken him.

With no further hesitation, he threw himself against the shutter. It gave with surprising ease. He hit the floor and rolled to his feet, sword in one hand and throwing dagger in the other. Confusion hit him, and vertigo ripped at him like a tempest. He fell to one knee, his weapons heavy. He could barely lift his head to see a low fire in the center of the room, and a guttering candle on a table against the far wall. Elnya was tied to a chair beside it, three men crowding around her, now looking at him.

Three men.

Two jumped at him. One was big, a massive brute like a bull. This Bull struck Caspan with a closed fist, knocking him back. The second one was thin as a twig, a spindly terror with a long, thin sword. Spindly stayed just out of reach, sword at guard, as Bull's arms wrapped around Caspan, pinning him from behind against the wall with both strength and sheer weight.

He felt groggy, and not from Bull's fist. He couldn't focus or muster his strength. Elnya seemed no better. She appeared unconscious, but with her peerless, green eyes open. Caspan saw her breathe, but she didn't move or react to the blade at her throat held by the third man. That one had the cold eyes of a killer. They burned into Caspan. Killer spoke, but Caspan didn't know the language. Killer tried again.

"Drop your sword."

Caspan played dumb. He smelled the stink of Bull's breath, hot against his ear.

"You know the Andravan language," Killer said. "You are Caspan Trey, the one this witch hired to protect her. Where's your desert-louse?"

"You can walk out of here," Caspan said. "You leave her be, and you have my word I won't harm you. Walk away."

Killer smiled. "If you don't drop your sword, I'm going to spill this witch's blood. You can try to kill me after that. It won't matter."

Bull and Spindly didn't talk. Killer was the leader. Caspan swallowed. His gaze swept around the room. What of the fourth man? Where was he? Had Terqmar been mistaken?

"I put down my sword, what's to stop you from cutting her throat?" Caspan asked.

"You're sword isn't stopping me now." Killer pressed the knife against Elnya's neck.

His strength failed. His will failed. He had lost. Caspan dropped his sword, ready to take his chances.

Before he spoke, the door burst inward. Terqmar leaped through the portal, his cane without its ornate head in his left hand, a thin bladed sword with a pommel in the shape of the cane's head in his right. Before he moved any further into the room, an object fell from the ceiling and onto him, throwing him to the ground.

The fourth man had appeared from the darkness like a ghost. As that Ghost wrestled with Terqmar, Caspan strained against Bull. Caspan's head slowly cleared, his strength returning. He swung back with his head, feeling it connect, hearing the snap of a breaking nose and Bull's pained grunt.

Killer slid his knife along Elnya's throat then pushed her and her chair over.

Frozen, Caspan could only bellow his rage. He watched blood spray out of her as Elnya hit the ground. Those bright green eyes that had burned into him in the market lost their lustre. Gore spattered her dark cheeks.

The strength of Bull's grip increased, but it couldn't hold him. Fury welled up in Caspan, burning through his limbs. He sensed rather than felt the knife. Grasping it, he twisted, and turned to face Bull. He drove the knife into Bull's chest. Bull sagged on top of him and he threw off the man's body.

Spindly advanced, drawing his sword back for a lunge. Caspan pulled his dagger out of Bull and threw. Spindly dodged aside. It gave Caspan time to dive for his sword. He turned on

Spindly. Killer advanced, bloody knife dropped beside Elnya's body. The sword in his hand had dark paste along its edges.

As though uncertain, Spindly stood before Caspan, sword weaving patterns in the air. Caspan did not wait for him. Spindly weakly parried Caspan's thrust. Caspan rammed Spindly aside with his shoulder, knocking him off balance. Caspan surged forward. Killer parried two thrusts, but a riposte ripped through his side. As he staggered from that, a downward stroke caught him in the chest. He fell.

Terqmar had wrestled free of his Ghost. The two circled each other warily. Caspan turned on Spindly. He drove his foot up into Spindly's groin. Spindly squealed. Caspan swung. Caspan's blow had such savagery it knocked aside the sword and tore a chunk out of Spindly's shoulder. Grunting, Spindly staggered back, and Caspan drove his sword into the man's belly. He groaned and reached out, trying to clutch at Caspan. The next stroke took off his head.

Caspan was ready to take Ghost's life as well. He didn't get the chance. Terqmar had already spit his opponent on his own thin blade.

Caspan and Terqmar stood silently among the five bloody, unmoving bodies. Terqmar wiped the blade of his sword on his dead opponent's cloak, and then slid it back into the cane. He sighed.

"I'm sorry. I failed you, and I failed her." Terqmar squatted over Elnya. "It was their ceremony. It robbed me of my power as it robbed hers. I underestimated them and their magic. Focusing on you disrupted their spells and gave me my chance."

Caspan shook his head, his eyes fixed on Elnya's body. She had not struggled, had made no sound or movement when the knife had opened her neck. She could not have felt it, could not have been conscious. Blood covered the entire floor, the life of five mixing there and spilling into the hall. Caspan still did not move.

Terqmar rose. "You did what you could. You did more than any could have expected."

He had failed before, had been unable to fulfill a contract. He had seen people die, even people he had been paid to protect. Never had he felt so empty. He could not imagine opening the door and leaving the building. His mind could not encompass the sunrise of a new day.

"But why her?" Caspan didn't know whom he asked. He didn't ask Terqmar, and he was the only other living person there. "Why a charm-seller in the Old Bazaar? Why an innocent young woman?"

"You did not know Elnya of the Old Bazaar well." Terqmar's sightless gaze rested on Elnya's body. "Nor did I. She may have had power she hid. She had connections I did not know of. If my own benefactor protected her, she must have had some potential. I doubt anyone knew the extent of her magic."

He walked to the back door. Just inside of it, he paused and looked back at Caspan. "You still have your silver. Use it to find yourself a solid roof under which to sleep. That shed of yours holds back neither wind nor rain." Terqmar looked out into a night ready to become morning. "You have done a great service to a great many people, killing these Witch-Finders. I would not doubt there are some willing to show their gratitude."

Caspan nodded, his gaze tied to Elnya's lifeless form. "I hardly knew her. I knew her face, every curve of her body, but I didn't know *her*. I never will."

Terqmar stood silently. Caspan could hear the breath catch in the other man's throat. Perhaps he had thought to say something, something to ease the pain, but realized how empty any platitude would prove.

"What worth silver?" Caspan slid his sword into its scabbard. The blood gathered around the hilt and slid down the sides of the sheath. He knew the damage to the blade that could cause. He didn't care. "If you need me, you'll know where to find me."

- the end -

Of Shadows and Flutes

I could bend your ear with tales of woe regarding the genesis of this tale, but self-pity is admirable in no one, so we'll pass on that.

Instead of woe, let's talk inspiration, because part of the background on this story is my admiration for the director Walter Hill. I actually enjoyed Walter Hill's work long before I knew who he was. I loved the movies the Warriors and 48 Hours. I can't say I loved Streets of Fire, but I certainly enjoyed it. By the time Wild Bill and Last Man Standing came around, I knew the director. I can't say I've loved all his work, but every film by him that I've seen has entertained me.

And this story came about as a bit of an homage to the first Walter Hill movie I ever saw: the Warriors. In the Warriors, a gang has to find its way back across New York over the course of one night while every other gang is the city is out to kill them because of a murder for which some weasels framed the Warriors.

And so here we have Decamaris, a figure who must traverse his own city while every other gang is out to kill him because of a murder for which some weasels frame him. It's not exactly the Warriors, but it hits all the beats. I hope it's as enjoyable for you as that movie was for me.

If you want to get into business talk, this is a story that I have not "shopped around." I have not attempted to sell it. It was written for a specific purpose—and I won't lie to you, that purpose was not this collection. However, when the situation changed and it no longer had a home, it lay dormant. It slept.

A story should never sleep. It should either be in the middle of a transformation—an edit, a complete rewrite, pieces of it being removed to be recycled elsewhere—or it should be in the middle of the submission process somewhere. When a story is ready—and the art is in judging when it is ready, an art I have not necessarily mastered—out it goes. If it is rejected, either fix it or send it back out. Don't let it languish.

But I'm lazy. It's my greatest failing, especially as a writer. So this story languished, but no longer. It has found a home. It's not a loss but it is not exactly a win. I should have had this circulating. I should have worked to market this story, get it in front of editors—or at least slush readers. That I didn't is a loss.

That you are reading this, and therefore are likely to be reading the story itself, is a win.

Of Shadows and Flutes

Decamaris stood outside the circle of illumination cast by the bonfire. Silently, he watched and listened as the man calling himself Laersun whipped the crowd into a frenzy with his visions of a union of thieves, a great guild that would take a place of power in the city. No one stood near Decamaris. Wrapped in shadow as much as in cloak and hood, he watched and waited. Across the bay, the lights of the Reach winked and twinkled, beckoning. Above, clouds blocked the stars and moons. A great storm approached, on this all the weather witches agreed.

The wind moved through the common forest that covered most of the peninsula between the village on Beacon Hill, at the north end of the Horn, and the one at Bridgend, in the south. It didn't have strength enough to drag away the words that blustered through it. Decamaris considered that unfortunate.

Laersun's harangue became more impassioned. He might be a speaker, but he wasn't a leader. He was a nobody. He ran a small gang in an unimportant quarter of the Reach. How had he gathered so many cutpurses and cutthroats? He didn't work alone. Someone was behind him. Someone with money and with power. Decamaris had tracked down Laersun, had found the meeting, now he needed to follow the money. Who had hired Laersun, who fed him his cues? And was there more beyond that? Levels and layers. Nothing in that city was simple.

Without a question, this pack of dogs had welcomed him, thinking Decamaris a representative of the Shadows' League. Only fools made assumptions. Though he bore the twin silver daggers that marked him as having completed the Twelve Trials, Decamaris wasn't from the League. It thought him dead. Would any even recognize Decamaris as an old comrade? Unlikely. Decamaris didn't even recognize his own craggy face, and short, dark, graying hair.

The crowd became wild. Laersun had reached them, or at least some of them. Wine and narcotics had reached the others.

Laersun spoke of creating a force that could challenge the Guilds, maybe even the Tribune. Dangerous talk, that. It wouldn't last long. Decamaris readied the dart. He covered it in shadow. Small, but tipped with a special toxin, its enchantments would destroy it soon after it broke skin. Hopefully, no one would know Laersun had been attacked, only that he had collapsed.

A smell reached Decamaris, something more than wood smoke, sea salt and unwashed bodies. Something touched his mind, made him nervous. He put his hand on his sword. A flash blinded him for a moment. He crouched, sword out at defense. The blade Scorpius, forged in an unknown age, covered in mysterious sigils, and bearing puissant enchantments, chilled the air.

Decamaris' vision cleared. Laersun lay on the ground, a dagger lodged in this throat. Decamaris took a step forward, but paused. Between him and the body stood a man hidden behind induced darkness. Decamaris saw through it, as he saw through all darkness. The man—a stocky fellow in a tattered cloak—met Decamaris' eyes. Tatter-cloak's face went ashen, his jaw dropped. Decamaris smiled. *Oh yes, I see you.* Scorpius sang a quiet, wailing song anticipating the slaughter.

But Tatter-cloak had friends. A motley bunch of hairy, scarred and ragged cut-throats massed around him, like infantry awaiting the charge. One of them, a thin, weasel-faced block of flesh, gave Decamaris a smile.

"Assassin!" Weasel pointed at Decamaris as he shouted his accusation. "The assassin killed Laersun. He's from the League."

"You gelded son of a poxed alley-whore." Decamaris readied a lunge. He would remove Weasel first, then bury the rest. Tatter-cloak would live long enough to tell Decamaris all he wanted to know.

The shouted accusations, though, had reached some in the crowd. While most panicked, fled or jabbered nonsense, a few took notice. In a heartbeat, a mob formed. Decamaris saw his blood in their eyes. A handful of dirty thugs didn't worry Decamaris. A mob, though, gave evil odds. One lucky stroke, one trip over an out-stretched leg, and Decamaris wouldn't see morning. His ill-ease reached Scorpius. The air around the single-edged blade wavered with distortion, as though it emanated great heat.

"I didn't kill Laersun, it was that jackal," Decamaris said. The mob didn't listen. Tatter-cloak and his gang had already begun to disappear into the crowd. "Fine then, reap what you sow."

The mob didn't have the courage to charge him yet. The sword in his hand, shining with its own pale, bluish light and his very appearance kept them scared. That wouldn't last long. The breaking point would come, and they would fling themselves at him thirsting for violence. His luck had proved sour that night. He decided to change it. Had he a grandmaster's powers, he could have called forth a fearsome shade. That, he couldn't do. He had, however, studied in Far Wall before he took the Twelve Trials. He didn't need one of the greater shades of the netherworlds when an illusion would serve his purpose.

Using his free hand, he sketched ancient runes in the air. "*Imago immanis somnitis.*"

Better than any other there, Decamaris knew the appearance a dreadful shade would take. With a minimum of concentration, he created the illusion of one. It spilled forth from his sleeve and sat there, gesticulating but silent, all sinewy darkness and cold. It did what Decamaris needed. The mob surged back. Decamaris ran. Flat out. It had been a long time since he had needed to retreat from anything. Discretion, though, met his needs.

Tatter-cloak and his gang would retreat as well. Decamaris needed to get his hands on them before they went to ground. He couldn't return from this hunt empty-handed, not with his quarry tagged by another. But to where would they retreat? Would they head north, to the Horn's Tip Beacon and Beacon Hill? South to Bridgend and passage to the city? Would they just disappear into the common forest? Doubt caused a moment's hesitation, but Decamaris couldn't allow delay. An assassin covered in magical shadow, striking after a blinding flash, it smelled of Far Wall.

Far Wall pointed to the Janus, the bogeyman wizard of the underworld. Far Wall had no gangs of its own, the wizards did not allow it, but would one of them dabble in such matters beyond the confines of the Guild Arcanis? Wizardry and criminality, a mixture sure enough to spark.

He followed his gut. Far Wall. That meant they would need to get into Old City. They needed to cross the bay.

More than simple revenge motivated his pursuit. Tatter-cloak had both destroyed his plans and set the blame on him. Were Decamaris to square things with his employer, he'd need to both exact retribution and acquire intelligence.

Tatter-cloak and his gang had a good head-start. They disappeared through the crowd. Decamaris had to skirt the gathering of criminals or face possible opposition. Opposition, no matter how weak, meant delay. Decamaris didn't need that. The clouds seemed to thicken, hiding the night sky. Had Laersun—or whoever ran Laersun—chosen that night for its deep dark? It did not matter. Darkness was Decamaris' home. He pulled it close around him, feeling safe. He could see in the inky black as though under a noon day sun.

He heard the mob swell behind him. There would be trackers among them, trackers that could follow even him. If this were a gambit of one of the powers in Far Wall, if this were the Janus' doing, those hunting him might have supernatural means— ethereal hounds and spirit coursers. They wanted his head. He couldn't afford to give it to them.

He hit the bay, the crowd of thieves somewhere behind him. The water crashed and roared, breaking against the rocky shore, heralding the coming storm. He saw a small boat bouncing through the bay, figures crouched low in it. Two pairs of oars cut the water, lazily propelling the boat to the opposite side, to the Reach. The lantern that hung from its prow might have caught another's notice. To Decamaris' shadow-piercing eyes, it burned like a flare, illuminating Tatter-cloak and his boys making their escape.

Decamaris had no boat. He was fairly certain he couldn't walk on water. He didn't try. That left Bridgend.

He followed the rough and craggy coast south, toward the natural stone outcropping that provided the link between the peninsula of the Horn, and the city proper. The only road ran along the plateau that topped the stone outcropping, guarded by watchtowers at either end.

The shouts of the hunt fell behind.

The boat had passed the midpoint of the bay between the Thumb and the Reach when Decamaris arrived at Bridgend. He paused for a moment to catch his breath. He needed to get past the watchtowers unseen. On such a cloudy night, with moon- and starlight so sporadic, that shouldn't prove a challenge.

The village stretched out from the towers like spilled blood. It had no regularity, no main street. It suited Decamaris well. While light leaked through the shutters of some structures, darkness enveloped Bridgend just as it did Decamaris.

Behind him, he saw no sign of pursuit. He saw no lights, no movement, and could hear no voices. Even over the crashing waves, he would have heard them.

No one guarded the watchtowers or watched the bridge once the sunset gong had sounded. Bypassing the wall offered little challenge. It only stretched down to the water. He could get past that as many others had, by wading through the bay.

He began a slow jog, intent on reserving his energy, but knowing the boat would cross to the Reach long before he could. The gates on the Reach side of the bridge were open. The watchtowers boasted no greater alertness than at Bridgend. Decamaris simply walked through.

The lantern on the boat's prow still burned, and that led Decamaris to it. Tatter-cloak and friends had dragged the boat a good ten strides up the shore, leaving it overturned. The trail was cold. Had Tatter-cloak and company traveled deeper into the

Reach? Had they turned north, south? Did they have some destination that night or had they gone to ground?

He heard the footsteps, though obvious care had gone into silence. By the sounds he counted five, moving slowly, uncertain. They approached him from the rear. He maintained a facade of searching the boat, waiting for those footsteps to get within Scorpius' reach. They didn't. Decamaris dropped his pretence and turned. The five who faced him looked hungrier and dirtier than Tatter-cloak's gang. That pretty much made them the saddest looking group of toughs Decamaris had ever encountered.

That was saying a lot.

"They're gone." Tall and lanky, with a long face and long, greasy dark hair, the speaker had more assurance than the others, though not by much. He kept the fear out of his voice. *Good for him.*

"I saw that." Decamaris took two slow breaths as he sized up the competition. "Where did they go?"

"They said there was a bounty." Lanky nodded toward the peninsula. "Some guy got killed over on the Horn. They said there was gold, we get the killer."

That didn't sound good. Decamaris tapped the side of the boat. "They said?"

"That's what they said." Lanky's smile had precious little white and even less compassion. "They said it'd be a guy all in black, like something out of the Shadows' League. They said he'd have a fancy sword."

Decamaris didn't want to kill these five. It might be a mercy for them, but Decamaris avoided killing out of hand. He had pity for Lanky and his pathetic little crew. "Did they tell you who this shadow murdered?"

The question made Lanky pause. "They said there was some big meeting, a bunch of the big gangs. The guy who got killed had organized the meeting."

"Of course, a big meeting," Decamaris said. "You guys are from the Reach, right?"

"Yeah, this is our ground." Lanky's assurance had begun to evaporate, as had his hostility.

Decamaris spread out his arms. "And were you at the meeting? Did you hear about a meeting?"

Lanky looked among his four comrades. None of them seemed too certain. None of them appeared ready to commit violence. None of them answered.

"So, there was a big meeting of all the gangs, just not you." Decamaris paused, but still no reaction. "And a Shadows' League assassin killed the big leader, so now there's a promise of gold for you all. Do you want to hear another story? Fat boy in a raggedy old cloak and his weasel-faced friend try to get into some action I had cooked up on the Horn. He and his gang completely screw up, get one of my boys killed, hurt another, then steal an old boat to get back here. After I took my man for help, I came here to get some retribution. How do you like that story? No big meeting, no big man, just a bunch of two copper cutthroats and a half-copper idea."

Lanky liked that story. "Yeah, it didn't make sense, a big meet of the gangs and no one mentioned it to us."

"Fat boy played on your good natures." Decamaris produced a minted talar of silver. "I'm playing on your common sense. I'd appreciate it if you pointed me in the right direction."

"They were headed down toward the Plaza of Unheard Whispers," Lanky said. "Heard one mention something about the Goose and Gown. There's a place called that down in Ditchrun, near the Old City wall."

Decamaris tossed Lanky the coin. "Ditchrun it is. Been a pleasure, gentlemen."

He didn't offer the five his back, though none made any threatening moves. None actually moved at all while he had them in sight.

A bounty—he wondered if that were true. True or not, Tatter-cloak passing that along could buy him some friends and buy Decamaris some trouble. Word would get around, word always got around when it came to coin, and his head would be looking like solid gold to the cutpurses of the Reach.

Laersun killed, Weasel-face placing the blame on him, and now maybe a bounty, but yet none knew his name. Still, were he to live through the night, there were those in the city who would guess his identity. Since he was supposed to be dead, that was bad.

The clouds above continued to thicken, cutting off the last vestiges of moonlight. Keeping to alleys and quiet streets, Decamaris moved quickly but with caution. He had to avoid the main streets. He had to pass unseen and silent. And when he reached the Goose and Gown? Maybe Scorpius would get to drink.

With careful steps, Decamaris approached the alley mouth. Beyond it, he recognized the Plaza of Unheard Whispers. A strange place, and one he would usually avoid, but the direct path lay through it. The many trees and shrubs would help to hide his passage, even though the plaza had six lanterns that forever burned—some gift from a Far Wall trickster. Past the plaza, another few blocks would get him into Ditchrun. Somewhere in there, near the Old City wall, he would find the Goose and Gown, and hopefully Tatter-cloak. If not, he would count this as one of the worst nights of his life . . . well, since he had "died."

Just as he stepped out of the alley, he froze once again. The street noises now carried something more. Some said that one could hear murmuring voices in the plaza, almost below the threshold of perception. Had he heard that, he would have been disturbed, but not particularly surprised. A pleasant tune from flute, harp, and a woman's singing, though, **that** he had not expected.

The ever-burning lanterns revealed three figures languidly draped on and around the plaza's trees. Decamaris did not know the tune, light and with a rolling lilt. He did know that he should avoid those three, carelessly performing to no audience save themselves, but he saw one flash a smile—a short, slim young woman with deliciously dark skin—and he ignored caution and sense.

"You travel late." The dark beauty held a flute, now silent, covered with intricate carvings.

Decamaris released what little darkness still clung to him and pulled back his hood. He did not move within reach of any of the three. "Perhaps I came to see you perform."

"Perhaps we are here to perform for you." The singer spoke with a voice that soothed like mulled wine in winter. Pale, fair-haired and pleasantly curved, she presented a tempting contrast to the flautist.

"If so, I count myself lucky," Decamaris said. "You sound delightful."

The harper—freckled, with bright green eyes and flowing red hair—stretched out against the tree, allowing Decamaris a fair view of her charms. "And how do we look?"

A low chuckle escaped from Decamaris. "Delightful."

"Would you like to hear more?" Flute took a step toward him. "Or would you like to see more?"

From a very young age, Decamaris had a sense for danger. He always listened, no matter the situation. He felt that tickle along the back of his neck. Singer's smile cracked, just for the briefest span, replaced by annoyance, perhaps impatience. Flute's tender sighs couldn't hide the tense muscles along her neck. Harper had her hand on something hidden beneath her cloak. Thoughts that would have shocked the mother he had never known passed from Decamaris' mind and his usual caution—some called it paranoia—reasserted itself.

"What I'd like is to walk out of here alive." Decamaris took a step back. While he couldn't conjure up a greater shade, he had an ally from the netherworlds. "*Umbra Umbris ades.*"

"I'm here, master." From out of the darkness smoked a slithering shadow. "Are we entertaining friends?"

"I really don't know." Decamaris pulled Scorpius a few fingers out of its scabbard.

Flute paused. Her eyes moved between the other two. Harper slid off the tree, her hand still beneath her cloak. Singer lost all artifice and scowled.

"Whatever it is you think you know, you're wrong." Decamaris slid Scorpius back into its home. "Whatever that tatter-cloaked pig told you was a lie."

"What pig?" Flute shook her head. "We heard through our regular sources, our wizard sources in Far Wall."

The mention of Far Wall caught Decamaris' attention. It made him think of the Janus again. What kind of game could he be playing?

Singer presented her empty hands. "Word is out on the wind. You're marked.

"We don't want to hurt you." Flute offered him a warm smile. "There's no need for that. Just surrender to us. Others won't be so kind."

That made Decamaris laugh. "I don't have time for this. I also don't want to hurt you, but I will." He drew Scorpius. The sword rivalled the six lanterns, its light no longer pale. The air around the blade shimmered and quivered. "You don't want to play that game with me."

The shadow hovered in the air in the midst of the plaza. It stretched to become a great, ogre-like shape with long talons and horns. "I've sent many a soul to hell for my master. It won't bother me to do it again."

Flute sagged, her arms limp at her side. "On your way, then." Her eyes, though, watched Decamaris from out of their corners.

Decamaris took a step, putting himself within reach. Flute lashed out, a blade seeming to have sprouted from her fist. Decamaris blocked the swing, bringing his arm up to catch hers. He slammed his elbow into her face. She fell back.

The other two rushed forward. Singer reached him, but Umbris blocked Harper. A tendril shot forth, touching Harper's chest. She stumbled back, hugging herself tightly. Singer had two long, thin blades, though she attacked with them as one. Catching her forearms with his own, Decamaris drove Scorpius' hilt into her temple. For a moment, only a moment, the distortion along the blade spread to cover her head. Decamaris stepped back, letting Singer fall to the ground.

Flute now stood, holding Harper. Harper's breath misted as she exhaled.

"My friend will reduce you to shells if you persist." Decamaris sheathed Scorpius, ignoring its complaints at being denied its due. He knelt down and touched Singer's throat. "She's alive. She'll be like this for two or three hours, but she'll awake no worse for it. You two best see to her."

Near where Singer had fallen, Decamaris saw Flute's instrument. In the scuffle, it had received its own wound. He picked it up, touched the long crack that ran most of its length. He tossed it to Flute.

Flute caught the instrument. "Now I owe you for this. That's reason to come after you."

"I'm sorry for it," Decamaris said. "If we cross blades again, I'll do what I must. Remember that."

Not showing his back, Decamaris moved through the plaza. He found his way into the darkness of an alley. Umbris came to him.

"You're being hunted?" Did a giggle actually come from that patch of nothing? "What have you done this time?"

"This time, I have done nothing." Decamaris quickly took in his surroundings. He and Umbris seemed alone, at least as far as he could tell. "I need to find a place with the sign of a goose and gown. It should be near the Old City wall."

The shadow's shape shifted back to that of a short man. "I don't have much time left, master."

Decamaris started off down the alley as quickly as caution allowed. "Use what time you have left. Find it for me."

The shadow disappeared into the night. Decamaris could feel the morning sun coming. He had little more than an hour of darkness left, nothing more. Darkness offered concealment and security. Darkness fed his confidence. The sun brought nothing but another day.

By the time the shadow returned, it had already begun to dissipate. "Two blocks forward, one block north. There's an inn. Goose and Gown." The shadow had time to say nothing more.

Two blocks and then one north. Decamaris broke into a run. Could Tatter-cloak have gone to ground in an inn? That wouldn't end the night well. Umbris had gone, and he couldn't return until after the next sunset. That left Decamaris, his pathetic little arsenal of spells, and Scorpius. Facing a common room full of drunks, sleepy though they might be, gave odds that the night would end with a dagger in his back.

With a glance at the next crossroads, Decamaris realized he had passed into Ditchrun. The Old City wall loomed large to the east. It had snuck up on him. He wasn't focused. He was getting tired, getting sloppy. Lost in his thoughts, he moved as though an automaton, one of those zombies he had seen in his younger days.

Decamaris continued through the alleys, moving toward the wall. Could the inn mark some secret passage, some way to bypass the wall? Surely the cohorts of the Tribune would know of such a breach. Surely.

Then again, never underestimate the power of arrogance.

He reached the end of the alley. Glancing up the street, he saw it; a three story structure not twenty paces from the wall. Out front of the solid-looking structure hung a board with a picture of a goose dressed in a magistrate's gown. Light shone from the windows and brought the sounds of merriment with it.

Decamaris paused. He could not bring the darkness with him in there. He had few choices. Should he wait, hope Tatter-cloak and his boys came out before morning? Should he enter the inn, perhaps in disguise, and ferret out his quarry? He didn't like either of those options. If the inn had a tunnel, or perhaps some magical portal that bypassed the wall, Tatter-cloak could be in Old City. From there, he could get to the wharves, to a ship that could take him up river or out to sea.

And if the Janus held Tatter-cloak's leash, he could get to Far Wall through Old City.

Decamaris couldn't risk it.

He saw no movement on the street, though a few carousers exchanged loud declarations just outside the inn. He crossed the street and followed a small passage between two buildings that shared frontage with the inn. He came out behind the row of structures, facing the wall.

A single, small lantern provided the only illumination, so the two men flanking the rear door would not likely see Decamaris. He, however, had no such difficulty. He hugged the building, taking a few careful steps toward the inn.

Two men, likely armed, though not particularly alert. Hardly a challenge. He marked the air with invisible runes. "*Iam dormitis.*"

Both men dropped to the ground. They uttered no sound, save the impact of their bodies in the dirt. The men at the front of the inn continued to shout at each other, but Decamaris heard nothing more. He waited a heartbeat, then two. Nothing. He glided to the door, his hand on Scorpius, ready for a trap. He paused before he reached the men. Their breathing came slow and deep. He advanced on the door.

The sound reached him before the movement registered. He danced back, away from the seeking hand. The two 'sleeping' men stood, smiles on their faces, weapons sliding out from beneath their cloaks.

"You had best be on your way." The speaker had a light build, but his arms showed cords of muscle and plenty of tattoos. His long nose looked like it had been broken a few times. "You get one warning, nothing more."

They gave him all the time in the world. Confidence. He hoped it wasn't warranted. "You guys aren't the regular guards, I take it."

"We are as regular as is required by this establishment." That one had thick arms and thick neck. His jaw looked strong enough to snap the serrated blade in his hand. "There is nothing within valuable enough to compensate you for your death."

The two split, moving to either side of Decamaris. He circled them, trying to keep both at his front. How had they marked his arrival? If the spell had not affected them, they shouldn't have even noticed it. He could only think of one thing: an item enchanted to alert them to magic. But they even knew how to react, as though they knew the form and purpose of the spell. Powerful magic there.

And that, once again, pointed to Far Wall, pointed to the Janus. Decamaris began to seriously consider just walking away. He had his limits.

"I'm not here to rob anyone." Decamaris continued to circle as he spoke, though he didn't reach for Scorpius. "I'm looking for a crew of thugs, led by a fat boy in a raggedy old cloak and his weasel-faced friend."

Tattoo-arms glanced at the door they had guarded then back to Decamaris. "That's too bad. You're going to need to speak to the boss."

"You don't want to push this any further." Decamaris knew nothing he said would dissuade them.

"Our apologies, but we don't have a choice." Thick-jaw gestured at Decamaris. "If you come quietly, there will be no need for violence, but I doubt that will be the case."

Decamaris pulled back his cloak, revealing Scorpius' hilt. "Smart boy."

Thick-jaw charged in first, sweeping down with his sword. Decamaris met it with a trilling, exultant Scorpius. Thick-jaw's sword rang off Scorpius, the impact making him stagger back. Decamaris felt none of it. Tattoo-arms had a mace in each hand, spinning them in linking circles, the two bludgeons almost intersecting but never meeting. How to get a blade past them? Decamaris lunged forward, dropping and rolling, knocking Tattoo-arms off his feet. Decamaris rose first, just in time to block another thrust from Thick-jaw. Scorpius beat off Thick-jaw's attack, and Decamaris' boot connected with Thick-jaw's codpiece. It struck metal. Thick-jaw smiled. He got Scorpius' crosspiece on that thick jaw for his troubles.

The distortion swept over Thick-jaw's face, it covered his head, and his eyes rolled back as he collapsed.

Never underestimate the power of arrogance indeed.

Decamaris had no time to savour the victory. He danced away from Tattoo-arms' double maces. While not graceful, Tattoo-arms was fast. He beat on Scorpius mercilessly. Scorpius had the reach, but nothing slowed Tattoo-arms' attack. Decamaris saw anger in the man's eyes. Did he think Thick-jaw dead? How close were these two?

Though Scorpius absorbed most of the impacts, some jarred through Decamaris' arm. Given time, he might get through Decamaris' defenses, get one lucky blow, maybe break an arm or a leg—maybe even crack a skull.

In one quick motion, Decamaris had a long, fighting dirk in his hand. Blocking with Scorpius, he jabbed with the dirk. Tattoo-arms broke his attack for a moment. He retreated. Decamaris stood his ground. Tattoo-arms gave him a moment, and Decamaris dropped the dirk. That confused Tattoo-arms, just as Decamaris hoped. Decamaris drew out the dart he had prepared for Laersun and threw. Tattoo-arms seemed to register it just before it pierced his eye. He fell forward, doing nothing to soften the impact.

Immediately, Decamaris searched Tattoo-arms for something to explain their reaction to his spell. It didn't take long. A stylized silver pendant in the shape of a double-sided mask hung from his neck by a dark leather cord. Decamaris snatched it off him.

He felt the presence of another just as the flash blinded him. An impact threw Decamaris back. He rolled with it, coming up on one knee. Perhaps because he held the pendant, perhaps it was the connection with Scorpius, but his vision cleared quickly. Cloudy, wavering, he could make out a circle of maybe ten figures, with him at its centre. He swept out with Scorpius, mimicking blindness.

The tableau froze. No one charged him. No one tried to put the knife in. His vision cleared completely. He saw Tatter-cloak. He saw Weasel-face. He saw the same motley bunch of hairy, scarred and ragged cut-throats he had seen on the Horn. With them, stood another figure. Tall and lithe, a cloak and hood covered it completely. A white mask covered the figure's face. He wore the same kind of stylized pendant as Tattoo-arms had.

Decamaris rose. "You'd be the Janus."

The figure tapped the side of its head with a single finger. "I am. And you?" Its voice, neither masculine nor feminine in tone, had a distracted, detached manner.

"Are not." Exerting his will, Decamaris dimmed Scorpius, though he could feel its displeasure.

"So be it, Mr. Nobody," the Janus said. "I am not here to harm you. I do not wish conflict with the Shadows' League."

So, the Janus believed Decamaris represented the League. *Useful.* "Conflict? Did you not put the bounty on my head? Did you not seek to kill one of the League?"

What came from the Janus sounded half-way between a titter and a chuckle. "I only meant to stall you, not harm you. Surely none of the obstacles in your path could have truly threatened you."

Obviously, the Janus overestimated Decamaris, but why admit as much? "What of Laersun?" Decamaris let his eyes wander over the opposition. Too many to be certain, but he might have a chance.

"An upstart." The Janus sniffed. "To think, speaking of uniting the thieves under his control. He was a nobody, a back-alley pimp from the Reach."

"Who ran him?" Decamaris asked.

"Who indeed." One finger tapped the Janus' mask on the chin. "Why would the League care?"

Decamaris held Scorpius loose, not threatening yet ready. "Such a naked power play unsettles the dynamics."

"Indeed." Again, that half-titter, half-chuckle from the Janus. "If you discover who is behind it, I will be most appreciative."

"And now?" Decamaris permitted Scorpius' light to grow, if only slightly. Tatter-cloak and company moved back a pace. "You've inconvenienced me plenty."

"You seem very determined to inflict violence on my people," the Janus said. He allowed time for a response. When one did not come, he stretched out an arm, empty hand open. "What if I drop the bounty? What if I put out the word that Laersun's assassin was killed? It would not implicate the League. It would not implicate you, per se. Would that be helpful?"

"Quite." Decamaris didn't lower his guard. Not yet. "You do that, and I forget I ever saw Tatter-cloak and his crew?"

"Tatter-cloak?" The Janus turned to survey the gang. "Ah, yes, you forget about him and his gang, and everyone else involved on the Horn."

Decamaris took a couple of steps toward Weasel-face, whose face turned pallid, eyes wide. "Agreed, with one stipulation."

"No deaths." For once, the Janus' voice carried real command. "I will accept no deaths."

"Of course." Decamaris swept out with Scorpius, slashing Weasel-face on the cheek, a gash that hurt and would scar. "No deaths." He punched Tatter-cloak in the face.

Second only to the Admiral among the Tribune's intelligencers—known within their number as the Admiralty—subordinates called him Teacher. Many called him worse when they thought he couldn't hear, but he heard everything. If a tick passed gas in the city, Teacher knew about it.

He sat at a table beside a shuttered window in a small, rented room at the back of the House of Red Silks. Men passed unseen through brothels. Secrets, they passed through brothels as well. He only paid coin for secrets, never for the other offerings.

Decamaris stood just inside the door, waiting for Teacher to notice. After a few heartbeats, Teacher turned in his chair. He did not evidence surprise, he simply gestured to the chair across from him

Letting the shadows fall away from him like water, Decamaris lowered his hood. He collapsed in the offered chair. Teacher filled his cup with wine.

"My thanks." Decamaris drank deep. "Not a good night. I have met the Janus. He . . . it is real. I still don't know who—"

Teacher raised his cup in salute, interrupting Decamaris. "We found Laersun, as intended."

Decamaris filled his cup again. "But Laersun was dead."

"We have those that can make even the dead talk," Teacher said. "Obviously all did not go as planned, but success isn't questioned." Teacher dropped a purse heavy with coin on the table. "Your fee."

The purse disappeared into Decamaris' voluminous cloak. "The League will hear of the night's events. It will put two and two together."

Teacher waved off the comment. "And get three. The League is not a problem, not now. It was Janus, then, that ran Laersun?"

"It was the Janus that had him killed," Decamaris said. "Professional rivalry, apparently."

"Professional, was it?" Teacher rose, the meeting done. "Get some rest. When we have our answers, we may need you again."

"I'll be ready." Decamaris drained and refilled his cup. "You wouldn't happen to know where I can buy a nice flute?"

Teacher paused, his hand on the door. "A flute? What for?"

Unthinking, Decamaris dropped the mask he wore as much as the Janus wore his. He let a smile reach his face. "Not for what, for whom."

the end?